No Longer Strangers

Richard Stoll

ISBN: 978 - 1 - 326 - 95870 - 1

Distributed by Lulu Press Inc. (www.lulu.com)

Preface:

Jo's boss has sent her to Scotland to deliver a small package in Stirling. The errand is causing her considerable disquiet; not only has she been given a most unusual explanation for the need for this personal delivery but also ordered to stay on for a further week in the area for no apparent reason. The whole affair is really rather odd.

After working hard at university to achieve a good degree, Stephen is travelling to the Scottish Highlands in the hope of walking off his disillusionment with mathematics by hiking up the West Highland Way to Fort William and beyond.

These two young people could not possibly have imagined that something as mundane as spilling coffee would lead to life-changing experiences for both of them. The trouble is they do not believe in miracles.

Note:

The West Highland Way is a hiking trail that goes from just north of Glasgow to Fort William at the head of Loch Linnhe. In places it uses sections of one of the Old Military Roads that were built in Scotland during the eighteenth century.

Cover picture: Glen Coe

Chapter 1: Unexpected Encounter

Stephen walked up the platform beside the 11:00 train to Edinburgh before boarding the second-class section and threading his way up the aisle of each coach in turn seeking a window seat. The rucksack on his back and coffee in hand – intent on seeping out from under the protective lid – did not help progress.

Unusually for him, he felt miserable. "It must be a reaction to all the hard work I've put in over the last three years or so," he thought. "On the face of it, I've every reason to feel happy…I've achieved my goal of first-class honours in applied mathematics…secured a good job starting in September…am off to hike in Scotland for the first time…but…I feel totally deflated and not even sure I like mathematics anymore!"

He had just entered the front coach when the train suddenly jerked into motion, causing him to bump into the end of a table between two pairs of facing seats.

There was an exclamation of alarm from the girl sitting in a window seat as her coffee wobbled precariously and several globes of liquid landed beside the cup.

"I'm so sorry!" he said apologetically, searching desperately for a paper handkerchief to mop up the spillage. The girl, however, had already produced one and was wiping the table with a scowl on her otherwise attractive face.

It was only then that he noticed the vacant seat opposite her; in fact, very surprisingly, she had the whole alcove to herself.

"May I sit here if I promise to replace your drink?" he asked hesitantly.

"Feel free," the girl replied, giving him a rather blank look, "but there's no need to get me more coffee; it's not particularly nice."

He smiled gratefully, stowed his rucksack and sat down carefully while the girl reverted to gazing out of the window at the rapidly passing London suburbs. "Her profile is quite delightful," he thought but was then surprised to see a solitary tear slowly rolling

3

down her cheek. A moment later, she gave a strange little swallow as if trying to hold back more.

Impulsively, he leaned forward and spoke very gently: "You look as unhappy as I feel. Would it help to exchange our problems? Sometimes things don't seem so bad when shared."

Startled out of her reverie, the girl looked annoyed and about to give him a sharp retort. Then her expression softened and she regarded him thoughtfully. It was a novel and rather disquieting sensation; attractive girls hardly ever gave him a second glance. In this case, however, he was aware that whatever this girl was thinking was giving her some reassurance that his motives were well meant and his suggestion was not some clumsy way of trying to pick her up.

"You're right; I am unhappy," she said at last. "I've been made redundant from the job I've had at an estate agent's office in Pangbourne for the last three years and I'm also worried about the final errand my boss has sent me to do in Scotland. Perhaps it would help to talk." She paused, waiting for his reaction.

"I'm really sorry about losing your job. It must be horrible to be told you're redundant," Stephen sympathized. "I know Pangbourne quite well, having just finished reading mathematics at Reading University. I often rowed up the Thames as far as there with the University Rowing Club."

To his surprise, the girl smiled. "I love rowing! I'm a member of Goring Rowing Club, although I won't be able to afford to carry on when my subscription runs out."

She frowned at the thought before continuing: "Money will be so short until I find another job that I'm even having to leave my rented bedsit in the village. When I get back from Scotland, the kind couple who were my foster parents until I was seventeen have offered me a bed while I sort myself out."

"That's kind of them," Stephen said. "You were lucky to be assigned to them. The fostering system is not always so successful, as I discovered after my parents died in an air accident when I was fifteen. Of course, I've lived in university lodgings and a hall of residence for the last three years. Anyway, enough about me, what's the problem with this errand of yours?"

The girl leaned forward and put her elbows on the table.

"Last Tuesday evening my boss asked me to stay behind when the office closed and offered me a bonus of two hundred pounds – to be paid into my bank account with my final June salary – if I would agree to spend a week in Scotland on an errand for a friend of his: a very eccentric retired Oxford professor. This man has just written a book containing some extremely erudite and innovative scientific ideas and wants an old student of his, now a professor at Stirling University, to review it before the final version is prepared. However, the author is so afraid his ideas may be stolen that he's written the document on a standalone PC and is not even prepared to risk transferring the PDF file over the web to this friend in Stirling. "Believe it or not," my boss told me, "he's actually prepared to pay the expenses of a courier to take the file in person. I've told him about you and that you might be pleased to have a pleasant week in Scotland. Are you prepared to go?"

"The £200 bonus sounded so attractive that I readily agreed. Quite a thick envelope was handed to me just after the office closed yesterday. I had expected something like a thin CD and so expressed my surprise. My boss explained that the book was stored on something called a mini-SD card in a protective plastic box. I've got to make the delivery to the professor's home in Stirling at seven o'clock tonight. My train ticket has been provided and a room booked and paid for in a B and B. I've also been given £350 in cash to cover another seven days doing anything I like, provided I stay in Scotland, but there's been no mention of bringing anything back at the end of the week!

"Well, I've been so busy getting ready to come away that I only started thinking about this strange errand when I was on the train to Paddington. Apart for the old professor's almost paranoid security fears, there are several odd things about it. First, why go to all this expense when the SD card could be sent by registered post? Secondly, if a human courier must be used for some reason, why the

5

need to stay in Scotland for a week after delivery? I haven't been asked to collect the card again. The third odd thing is that, while great care has been taken to plan my northbound trip, I've not even been supplied with a return ticket!"

"Yes, that is odd," Stephen said, looking puzzled. "Your boss doesn't seem to care what happens to you once the delivery is made but does want to keep you out of circulation for a week."

He pondered for a moment. "I wonder if we can get some clue from the PDF file itself. May I see the card?"

"Unfortunately, the envelope is sealed. Anyway, how can you read the contents?"

He gave her a triumphant smile as he opened a shoulder bag on the seat beside him and drew out a notebook computer.

"I can do most things on this; it has an 11-inch screen and is quite powerful for its size and surprisingly light. I won it as a prize for something I wrote; I could never have afforded to buy it! Most of my university work was done on an old 15-inch laptop."

In astonishment, she handed him a brown envelope wrapped in a sheet of A4 paper secured by a rubber band. The envelope was unmarked, but the paper bore the name and address of Professor S S Makin and a sketch map showing the location of both his home and the bed and breakfast accommodation that had been booked for her.

"You must keep this envelope and make sure you buy something similar in Stirling," Stephen said, as he carefully slit the top with a small penknife. They were both surprised when the only thing that emerged was the mini-SD card in its plastic case.

"Not even a brief greeting from an eminent professor to one of his old students!" he commented.

"Or even a word of thanks for the onerous task the poor man or woman is about to undertake," the girl added. "With a title like professor, I won't find out until I get to the house."

Stephen extracted the card and carefully slid it into a small slot on the side of his computer, tapped a few keys, and turned the screen towards her. Reduced in size to fit the height of the screen was the page of a book full of dense text interspersed with algebraic equations.

"I'll magnify the image so that we can read more comfortably," he said.

"It'll look like gobbledegook to me however large it is!" she muttered.

He scanned back to the beginning of the document and expanded the first page to display the top half at roughly full size.

"Apparently your professor's name is John C Kelly and there's a note inserted in italics at the beginning to say that he hasn't decided on the full title yet or written the introduction and this file only contains the main chapters. If you can give me two or three minutes, I'll scan through a few of the 428 pages."

Very soon, however, he became increasingly puzzled and looked across the table at the girl almost accusingly. "I thought you said this was a high-powered scientific text?"

Chapter 2: The Plot Unfolds

The girl raised her eyebrows. "That's what my boss told me. He said it contains some extremely erudite and innovative scientific ideas. I'm not clever enough to make up that description!" She looked rather upset that he doubted her story.

"Sorry – I didn't mean to imply that you were not telling the truth! However, all I'm seeing at the moment is an introduction to partial differential equations; the sort of textbook used by undergraduate mathematicians and scientists."

He continued to scan the document more rapidly and then gave a gasp: "I've just found something entirely different; the textbook stops mid-sentence at the bottom of one page and there are now pages of computer coding!"

He began to count very softly: "1, 2…8, 9…14, 15…23, 24 pages of code in total. Then the textbook carries on as if nothing has happened. This is extraordinary!"

He went back a few pages and pointed to the screen. The girl had come to sit beside him by now, too dumbfounded to speak.

"Most of it is written in a code called C++, but, as you move on, there are segments in a different language: FORTRAN I think. It was once popular in engineering but isn't used very often nowadays. There are a few lines of explanatory text at the beginning of the coding and also dotted around in various places, but it's all too technical for anyone other than an expert in the field to understand."

He looked at one of the pages more closely. "There's also something odd about the appearance of these pages; they're not as clear as in the textbook."

There was a pause. "Would you believe it? I think the original must be a printed document and some pages have been scanned to form JPEG images and then imported into the PDF file. That would have been quite a tedious job because each image has to be handled separately. I can only assume that a maths text was used as the hiding place because it's probably easier to find a free-to-download one on the web than something on advanced physics."

Stephen looked at his companion and smiled. "Nobody would normally search a long book for a hidden secret. It was a bit of luck that I looked at it and, being a mathematician, twigged that it had nothing to do with erudite and innovative scientific ideas!"

"What on earth do I do now?" the girl asked. "If that computer code has been obtained illegally, I'm in trouble! Are you sure the old professor didn't write it himself and this is yet another layer of paranoid security?"

"I suppose he could be hyper-cautious in the extreme! But why go to all this trouble? As the author of the code, it would be relatively easy for him to carry on with the task of getting the program to run successfully. It could be done on a good desktop PC with the appropriate compiler software. On the other hand, anybody else will find it a mammoth task. Anyway, if he is the author, why hasn't he got the original program file but only a printed version of it? To be any use, it will have to be typed into a computer all over again."

"Perhaps he wrote it years ago when he was still working in Oxford and now only has a paper copy that he wants this old student of his to resurrect on a more powerful computer," the girl suggested.

"I suppose that's just possible, especially as some of it is written in FORTRAN. In fact, it's the only possibility if we're not dealing with something criminal," Stephen replied, as he carefully removed the SD card from the notebook. "I suppose we must keep an open mind and give our professor the benefit of the doubt for now."

While the girl was tucking the card safely away, he searched through the pictures stored on his notebook and selected one.

"Before I get us both something to drink and we plan the next move, I need to convince you that I'm genuine," he said. "There seem to be too many coincidences: I live close to Pangbourne; I love rowing; I'm on the same train and going to the same destination. I could just possibly be a member of a rival gang trying to steal that piece of coding; after all, I've now managed to get a copy on my computer!"

He laid his Reading University Student's Union membership card and train ticket to Stirling on the table, at the same time pointing to a picture on the notebook screen showing eight oarsmen sitting in a racing boat with the coxswain endeavouring to keep a firm hold of the mooring post at the river's edge. Nine grinning faces were looking at the camera; one of them was Stephen.

The girl looked at him with a smile that lit up her whole face. "There's no need for all this proof; I never doubted you for a moment," she exclaimed. "We're friends now and my name's Joanna, but I much prefer Jo."

He relaxed visibly. "I'm Stephen," he said and they solemnly shook hands.

His hand tingled at her touch. "There's something really special about this girl. I even like the name Joanna," he thought, before pulling himself together.

"Let me get us a drink, or some soup, or both. What would you like?"

"A cup of soup would be nice, thank you: any flavour will do," Jo responded. "I'll treat you to some sandwiches later; we don't get to Edinburgh until 15:35 and only have about twelve minutes transfer time to get the Perth train to Stirling."

......

Fifteen minutes later, Stephen reappeared. "The choice was cream of chicken or tomato, so I got one of each. You choose."

She selected the chicken and they sipped the hot liquid in companionable silence until he apologized that it was so salty.

"I suppose we must expect that when it's made by squirting boiling water into a cup already containing the dry powder mix," she said. "But has the walk down the train given you any inspiration? I certainly don't want to be handling stolen goods, but if I fail to turn up at the address in Stirling my boss will be furious. My final month's salary is due to be transferred to my bank account sometime tomorrow and I can't afford to have it stopped. I know I'm being selfish!"

She looked at him rather forlornly and he came to a decision; he would offer to do something that might be quite tricky, but if it worked it would give her some breathing space.

"If this whole thing is a criminal conspiracy then the two professors are definitely involved. On the other hand, as you suggested earlier, it's just possible that the retired professor is a programming genius and has prevailed upon a longsuffering ex-student to do an immense amount of work for him in this secret way.

"This is my suggestion; you let me render the computer program useless by leaving several pages intact at the beginning and end but removing great chunks of vital coding in between. I can try to bulk out the file in some way to keep the total page count the same. I'll need at least twenty minutes in some quiet place to do the job. You can hand over the card as arranged. Hopefully, my tampering won't be noticed until the program is examined thoroughly.

"Later this evening, I'll have a closer look at the coding to see if I can spot any clues as to its origin. Then tomorrow we can track down the professor again, preferably at the university to make sure he or she really is a professor, and confess what I've done. Only if there's a totally convincing reason for this charade do we hand over the proper version. If not, we go to the police. What do you think?"

Jo looked at him in astonishment. "Are you really prepared to do all that to help me out?" she whispered.

"Of course I am. As you've said, we're now friends and that's what friends do," he replied.

"Then I think you're amazing and I accept gratefully," she said, giving him another of her genuine smiles. "When we get to Edinburgh I can 'phone ahead to the guesthouse in Stirling to see if they have a room for you. That would give you somewhere quiet to do the job before we set out to do the delivery."

......

Soon after Stephen and Jo had formulated this plan of action, the train reached its first stop at York. It turned out to be fortunate that the need for relative privacy was over because more passengers boarded the train and the aisle seats were now occupied.

It seemed entirely natural for the conversation to turn to their shared love of rowing and a happy time was spent reminiscing about past races and even the pleasure of practice sessions very early in the morning. It turned out that Jo was accustomed to sculling (using two oars) as a member of a crew of two or four, without a coxswain to steer, whereas Stephen was a regular member of his university's second eight.

"For some reason, I even relish having to inhale the mist that is sometimes on the water at that early hour!" he chuckled.

She smiled at the recollection but was less enthusiastic. "Yes, but you have a cox to steer you safely: we don't! We've had more than one near miss on a misty day. And you only have one oar to handle not two."

"At least you don't have a bossy cox shouting at you all the time!" he retorted.

They both laughed. "One day I'll challenge you to a single's sculling race if I can borrow two boats from Goring," she promised.

Stephen looked at her. Did she really mean it and want to continue seeing him after they parted in Scotland? A quiver of excitement passed through him. It was a pity that he was starting his job in Swindon at the beginning of September.

Aware that it would not be long before the train reached Newcastle, they asked their neighbours to keep an eye on their seats and rucksacks before making the journey down to the buffet car for sandwiches and coffee.

Standing in the queue, Jo asked her companion what work-outs he did as part of his fitness regime. "Of course, as an undergraduate, you've had access to much more equipment than I have," she said rather enviously.

They were so intent on discussing the benefits of this or that exercise that they were still doing so when they returned to their seats carrying sandwiches and coffee, although Jo was still feeling embarrassed because Stephen had paid with a £20 note before she had even managed to get her purse out.

......

In the end, it seemed no time at all before the train was pulling slowly into Edinburgh Waverley and the young couple alighted thankfully. Having checked which platform the train to Stirling would depart from, Stephen hurried off to get two cups of proper coffee from the Costa kiosk in the centre of the attractive concourse while Jo sat down to contact the guesthouse on her mobile. When he returned, she was looking rather distressed.

"I'm afraid the guesthouse is full tonight," she explained. "However, the landlady surprised me by saying that my room is a twin. She suggested my friend could share the room and pay the difference between single and double occupancy. When I hesitated, she added that it was en-suite! When I said I'd 'phone her back, she said not to bother but just turn up; there'd be no difficulty providing an extra breakfast if necessary. I'm so sorry!" She was now almost red with embarrassment.

Stephen, determined to set her mind at rest, spoke gently: "I'm quite prepared to share if it would help. I promise to behave myself and respect your privacy, which should be quite easy with the luxury of an en-suite. In a way, it would be safer if we stay together in case our tampering with the SD card is found out sooner than I expect. Your boss knows where you are tonight and so it would be easy to track you down. I'd certainly be happier if I'm on hand to support you."

Jo breathed a sigh of relief. "So would I," she whispered and gave him a smile full of gratitude. Even so, Stephen was glad that he had had the sense to use the word "support" and not "protect"; he did not want to alarm her, but there was a possibility that this gang – if indeed there was one – might react very unpleasantly after discovering their subterfuge had been thwarted.

13

Chapter 3: Stirling

As the train drew away from the platform on the rather slow fifty-minute journey to Stirling, only forty miles away, Stephen remarked: "We'll be stopping at Haymarket, Edinburgh's second mainline station in a couple of minutes. After that we must watch out for the famous Forth Rail Bridge."

"Yes, I've been looking forward to that experience," Jo said. "Apparently the bridge has been given a special preservative coating that will last for years and save the need for painting to go on in an almost endless cycle!"

A few miles later there was a rumble as the train entered the bridge. Some of the passengers craned their necks to see as much as possible of the famous structure: all one and a half miles of it.

"Victorian engineers certainly knew how to build!" was Stephen's admiring comment.

......

Fifty minutes later, they were consulting a tourist information map at Stirling station to find the roads in which the guesthouse and Professor Makin's house were situated.

"The university is nearly three miles northeast of the city centre on the A9," Stephen remarked. "To get to your addresses, we need to take the same road and turn left after just over a mile." He pointed to a long road that left the A9 and ran northwest.

"Let's walk after sitting for so long," Jo said, "but first we need a decent meal; it's four-thirty! The food is on me," she ended.

"There's no need; I can pay my share," he replied, as they walked towards the city centre.

"I insist. You're going to a lot of trouble on my behalf. If you hadn't met me, you'd probably been setting out on your hike immediately."

"No; I planned to see a little of Stirling first and leave early tomorrow. But I accept your kind generosity."

"Well, I'm going to delay your morning departure by the time we've seen the professor again and even more if we have to go to the police station."

She suddenly pointed to a restaurant on the other side of the street; it had a large notice in the window stating that a main-course buffet was available all day. "Look! All you can eat for a fixed price! That can't be bad; I could eat a horse!" she exclaimed, taking his hand enthusiastically to lead him across the road.

The action had to come to her without conscious thought. Suddenly realizing what she had done, she turned to him in slight embarrassment. He, however, was looking at her with a gentle smile and she felt strangely happy.

The buffet turned out to be a plentiful choice of both cold and hot dishes. At least two visits to the counter seemed to be quite usual, as several hungry students were demonstrating.

"Thank you for your generous hospitality," Stephen said to Jo as they left. "I feel set up for the rest of the day now!"

She looked pleased. "You're very welcome, but I must remember to buy a carton of milk to make a decent cup of tea later if the facilities are provided in the bedroom. The long-life milk provided is horrid in tea!"

Although it would have been nice to see a little more of the city, they were anxious to walk north immediately because Stephen was not sure how long it would take him to alter the contents of the SD card.

Just over half a mile later, they found themselves crossing the Forth. "It's shrunk enormously since the Edinburgh crossing!" Jo remarked.

"It was an estuary back there," was the reply.

"Sorry to be so stupid; I didn't realize that Edinburgh is almost on the coast!"

"Well, it's a good few miles inland from the open sea," he said to comfort her.

......

The guesthouse looked surprisingly nice as they approached it and the middle-aged woman who opened the door gave them a warm welcome. She did not seem even faintly surprised that the friend Jo had mentioned on the 'phone was male and ushered them to a pleasant room with a quiet outlook. Stephen was pleased to see that it had a dressing table you could actually sit at without knocking your knees.

As soon as they had settled in, he sat down and began work. He was so engrossed in what he was doing that he hardly noticed Jo place a cup of tea a short distance from his elbow.

At last he sat back with a satisfied grunt and sipped his rather tepid drink. "Finished at last, although it's taken me slightly longer than I expected. It's a good job I've got some excellent PDF editing software on this notebook. I've copied both the original file and the corrupted one to a spare flash drive for safety. Professor Makin may have been told to expect 24 pages of coding and so I've simply duplicated some of the remaining pages to match!"

"I think you're brilliant!" Jo said admiringly.

Stephen coloured slightly but only said: "If you can give me the SD card, I'll overwrite the file on it with my sabotaged version."

She solemnly handed him the card and watched for the few seconds it took to complete the transfer. Just as solemnly he handed it back for her to insert in the new envelope purchased in the city centre.

As they left the bedroom ten minutes later to walk to the professor's address, he explained what he had done. "I'm leaving my notebook locked in the wardrobe and keeping this flash drive in my pocket at all times. We can't be too careful. If we have to go to the police, I can leave it with them as evidence."

Jo linked arms with Stephen as they walked down the road and looked at him with a confident smile. He said nothing but within him surged a wave of warmth and tenderness.

A few minutes later they entered the end of the professor's road. "We need Number 26," Jo whispered.

"Well, we're standing beside 53 and so it's on the other side about half way down," he said. "I suggest we stay on this side and walk very slowly; we're three minutes early."

He was pleased to see that the road sloped gently down from the higher ground on which they were standing. This would enable the house to be watched from a good vantage point.

"I'd like to come with you but it would be safer if the professor doesn't know anything about me," he said. "If he happens to spot me keeping watch some distance away and quizzes you, please don't let on that I'm a mathematician or have anything to do with technical stuff. Pretend my subject is European history or something!"

Jo was sorry to have to go alone but could see the logic of his plan; it was vital for the professor to believe she was just an innocent courier doing a job of work.

The houses were widely spaced and looked prosperous. In fact, just the sort of property a university professor might be expected to own. There was even a grass verge between the road and pavement.

They came to one of the few trees that graced the verge on their side. "Excellent, I'll stop here." Stephen said. "Judging by the number of the house beside us, Number 26 is probably one of those two houses with the tall hedges a little further down on the opposite side. I'm just high enough up here to be able to see their front doors and so I can keep you in sight."

He squeezed her arm encouragingly. To his surprise, she reached up and gave his cheek a quick kiss.

"Geronimo!" she whispered bravely and left him.

Chapter 4: House Call

Stephen watched Jo cross the road and walk down the slope, checking the house numbers as she went.

"If the professor asks her to go inside, I'll give it five minutes before I follow," he thought. "It can't be helped if I blow my cover; I'm not going to let her come to any harm!" He was almost surprised at how protective he felt.

She paused outside a house, opened a gate set into the tall hedge and disappeared briefly before the top of her head appeared again. A few yards from the front door, however, somebody must have called out because she turned off the path and crossed the grass. The head of a man came briefly into view as he moved forward to greet her and it was clear that a discussion was taking place. Two minutes later, she moved back towards the gate and turned to make a farewell gesture before stepping out on to the pavement.

The spring in her step as she returned up the slope conveyed her sense of relief that the delivery had been completed. Stephen turned to march rapidly up his side of the road in case the professor decided to peer over the gate to make sure that Jo was really leaving. She realized what he was doing and did not cross the road to join him until they were safely out of sight.

"That went more smoothly than I expected," she said, face flushed with success. "The professor was pruning a rosebush. I must say he looked extremely professorial and was very polite. Fortunately, he didn't offer me a cup of coffee and so I didn't need to use the rather feeble excuse I'd made up to avoid going indoors. He did, however, ask if I'd been to the guesthouse yet and so he already knows where I'll be tonight."

She fell into step beside Stephen and linked arms with him. He looked down at her with a smile.

"You've done a difficult job amazingly well. I think you're very brave and it's a privilege to be your partner in exposing a possible crime. Anyway, I'm not letting you out of my sight until

18

you're safely out of Stirling and on your way to your chosen Scottish destination."

Looking surprised at the compliment, Jo beamed at him. "I haven't given my walking route much thought," she said slowly. "It can be anywhere that's wild and beautiful. Where do you suggest?"

"The Trossacks are very beautiful," Stephen said. "The town of Callander on the edge of that area is about twenty miles northwest of Stirling. You can get there on a No. 59 bus. I know that because I was planning to take it as far as a place called Blair Drummond before walking west to Aberfoyle and then circling northeast back towards Callander. It's a trip of less than 30 miles and passes two beautiful lochs.

"Then I was aiming to go up through the eastern edge of the Trossacks to Crianlarich and join the West Highland Way, a hiking route that runs all the way from just north of Glasgow to Fort William. From there, I was going to go on to Mallaig on the west coast opposite the island of Skye. I'll probably come back the same way as far Crianlarich but then continue down the West Highland Way through the central Trossacks to Glasgow, where I've already booked a ticket on a train to London around midday on Tuesday week. The Way runs down the eastern shore of famous Loch Lomond."

He looked at her and hesitated, not sure how she would react if he suggested they team up and travel together. He decided to take the plunge.

"What about joining me on the walk? I can point it out to you on my map over a snack and drink at a pub close to our guesthouse called The Birds and Bees? There was an advert about it on a notice board in the hallway."

She considered his suggestion for a moment and then a delighted smile spread over her face. "I'd love to do that, thank you. I'd also feel much safer with a strong companion; we still don't know the outcome of the "book that never was" saga!"

He could hardly contain his pleasure but managed to restrict himself to a happy, "Let's celebrate then!"

They march on energetically. Stephen admired the smooth fluid strides of the girl still linking arms with him. "It must be the result of all her rowing and fitness training," he thought.

......

The Birds and Bees turned out to be an attractive white building with tables outside facing an extensive area of open land on the opposite side of the road. They managed to find an empty table and sat down to consult the menu. Neither of them was particularly hungry after their substantial meal only three hours ago.

Jo spotted some nice-looking soup and crusty rolls being delivered to a nearby table and Stephen went inside to order it for both of them and get two cold drinks.

Nearly an hour passed enjoying the excellent soup and pouring over Stephen's large folding map that covered the Trossacks and the Western Highlands as far north as Fort William and Mallaig. He pointed out the elongated 30-mile loop he had mentioned earlier and then the route to and along the West Highland Way.

"If I won't be in your way and my money lasts out, I'd love to do the whole trip to Mallaig," Jo said. "I suppose I could then get a train most of the way back."

"Of course you won't be in the way! I'd really appreciate your company," Stephen assured her. "As to funds; if you're happy to continue with twin-bedded rooms, a half share should be less than the cost of a single room. I can also book you a cheaper ticket from Glasgow to London in advance on my computer as soon as you let me know the day you need to go, or you could wait until Tuesday week and travel south with me."

Jo shook her head sadly. "My money won't last that long."

"We'll see," he said and changed the subject by pointing to the map again. "The bus journey to Blair Hammond is about six miles. If we aim to stop for the night in Aberfoyle, we'll have a walk of 14 miles that'll take about four hours with a short stop for refreshments. I hope we don't get delayed too long in Stirling tomorrow morning!"

Just then, Jo's mobile emitted a tinny tune. "Who on earth can this be?" she muttered as she answered it. A second later, looking worried, she covered the mouthpiece briefly to whisper, "My boss!" Her face soon cleared, however, as she said: "Yes, I delivered it to him at seven o'clock, almost to the minute." The voice at the other end muttered something to which she replied, "Thank you! Bye."

Apart from the 'phone call, the evening was a great success. Not only was it pleasant sitting outside the popular restaurant looking out over the open land on the other side of the road but they were becoming increasingly relaxed in each other's company.

"Jo's really special!" Stephen thought, as he watched her enjoying the hot drink he had just bought. "I wish we'd met two years ago; to think that she only lives a few miles from Reading! It would have also prevented me making a fool of myself with my last girlfriend. I have the feeling that, if a really serious friendship with Jo starts, there's no turning back."

......

They left the guesthouse at 8:15 after a surprisingly good breakfast and walked back past the Birds and Bees on their way to the campus of Stirling University. Stephen had re-examined the computer program the previous evening while Jo was having a shower but without being able to spot any clues as to its origin or subject matter.

As they walked, Jo exclaimed: "After that breakfast, I'm set up to last all day, but the meal tonight is on me; you treated me to a lot yesterday."

"No I didn't; you bought our excellent buffet lunch!" Stephen objected.

"You've been such a help with my problem that I insist," she reiterated and immediately changed the subject by cheekily adding: "I slept so well I didn't even hear you snoring!"

"Huh, I don't snore! At least I hope not," he objected before realizing she was teasing him.

21

Then he noticed they were about to pass the turning leading to the road where the professor lived.

"We're within a couple of hundred yards of the professor's house," he said. "I suppose it would be sensible to see if he's still there. If he's gone to work, we can at least find out the name of his department and go straight to it."

Three minutes later, they were ringing the professor's doorbell. It took quite a long time before a rattle was heard and the door opened as far as the security chain allowed. A middle-aged woman peered at them through the narrow gap; she appeared to be clad in a dressing gown or what would probably be referred to as a housecoat in this up-market road.

"What do you want?" she asked crossly.

Stephen spoke as politely and apologetically as he was able. "We're sorry to disturb you but we need to speak to Professor Makin rather urgently. If he's already left for the University perhaps you could kindly tell us the name of his department."

The two young people were certainly not expecting the reply that emerged.

Chapter 5: The Plot Thickens

"There's no one of that name living here!" said the dishevelled woman as she began to shut the door.

"But I spoke to Professor Makin yesterday evening," Jo blurted out quickly. "He was pruning that lovely red rosebush." She pointed across the lawn.

To her relief, the woman hastily released the door chain and came out on to the doorstep looking totally bewildered.

"It was almost exactly seven o'clock and he had a small pair of secateurs in one hand and a rose in the other," Jo continued rapidly. "In fact, I remember thinking it was rather a shame because the petals had only just begun to fade."

The woman's expression had now added shock to bewilderment. "But we only arrived back from a short holiday in Malta late last night. This man had no right to be loitering in our front garden let alone touching my precious roses! Are you sure you have the right house?"

"Absolutely," Jo replied firmly and Stephen nodded in support. "I recognize your splendid beach hedge: the most attractive hedge in the road," he said.

"Well, I'm sorry I can't help you trace the wretched man but I'll get my husband to invest in a security camera after this episode!"

Stephen thanked her as they turned to walk back down the path. Politely opening the gate for his companion, he happened to glance at the base of the thick hedge; a dead rose and a couple of small clippings lay between two sturdy beech stems. He said nothing but hurried his companion out on to the pavement.

Taking her hand, he led her up the slight gradient at an even faster pace than on the previous evening. "That phony professor even had the cheek to toss a few rose bits under the hedge on his way out," he said crossly. "I'm kicking myself for not having had the sense to check online if a Professor Makin is listed as a member of the university teaching staff. I'm sorry!" He looked at her apologetically.

"Don't blame yourself; you've been a brilliant help," she assured him. "Without you, I'd have just been a gullible fool and delivered the goods as instructed. That wretched man looked the part and gave me no reason to think the house might not be his; he was as cool as a cucumber!"

"Yet he took a great risk that somebody in one of the neighbouring houses might see him. He must have been there at least ten minutes before we arrived," Stephen said. "What really puzzles me is how he knew so far ahead that the house would be unoccupied; it had to be before the address could be written on the sheet of paper you were given."

"That was only two days ago, although I must say it seems longer," she said as they re-emerged on to the road leading to the A9 and University.

Her words, however, had caused him to stop abruptly. "You've given me an idea!" he exclaimed. "I wonder if he lives in one of the other houses in the road. The holiday plans of Number 26 may be known by several neighbours. When we go to the police station, I'll suggest they ask that woman about her local friends and contacts. Meanwhile, we'd better check at the campus; any office there will have access to an internal telephone directory that lists all the members of staff."

They hurried on and soon arrived at the main road where they turned north. After walking almost half a mile, they were relieved to come to a roundabout where a large sign pointed to a road on the right leading into the extensive campus. It appeared to be spread over many acres of parkland because it was another two hundred yards or so before they came to the first large building – the Sports Centre. "There must be a reception desk in there able to help us," Stephen said. "Otherwise we'll be walking around forever!"

It helped that they were of student age; having explained what they were trying to find out, the helpful receptionist consulted an on-line directory. There was no member of staff with the name Makin, professor or otherwise.

"I suppose it was sensible to check, although it was already pretty obvious that the man is a complete fake," Jo remarked as they walked back towards the main road.

Just then they heard a university bus coming up behind them and slowing down to stop a few yards ahead. "It's going into the city. Let's see if it'll take us," Stephen called as they hurried up the pavement.

They jumped on after several students who all had travel cards; the driver rather reluctantly accepted cash payment. "This will save us half an hour," Stephen said as they found a seat.
......

Somewhat to their dismay, the visit to the central police station lasted for well over an hour, including the time taken for Jo to help a police artist produce a good likeness of the fake professor.

The sergeant who initially interviewed them upset Jo when he learned that the SD card had actually been delivered. "In my opinion," he said rather officiously, "you've come very close to committing an offence if it turns out that this computer software has been stolen!"

Stephen immediately assured him for the second time that, as a mathematician, he was perfectly capable of rendering the software useless.

Jo was grateful for the firmness in her companion's voice. "When I was asked to do the job, my boss went out of his way to stress the eccentricity of this elderly professor," she pleaded. "Stephen and I thought it just possible that he was the author of the software and going to ridiculous lengths to make sure it was not discovered. We needed more time to plan what to do. After all, we didn't discover the hidden code until not much more than four hours before it was due to be delivered."

Stephen sprang to her defense again. "Making the dud delivery at the appointed time has delayed the alarm being raised amongst the criminals; they'll have no idea it's been rendered useless until someone with programming knowledge examines it."

In the end, the sergeant found a young detective constable to take over. This was a great help because the man, about the same age as Stephen, was bright and intelligent and clearly intent on progressing quickly up the promotion scale.

It did to take long for him to hear the full story and their reasoning all over again and agree that they had taken a sensible course of action under the circumstances. He was particularly pleased when Stephen handed him the flash drive containing both the original and the corrupted PDF files. "I'll get this copied to the Thames Valley police immediately; they'll have to find out if we're dealing with industrial espionage or something worse."

He took the flash drive into an interconnected office and could be heard issuing instructions about the device to one person and asking another to check if a John C Kelly was a genuine retired Oxford professor.

When he sat down again, he said: "From what you tell me, it seems likely that we've got a few more hours before the criminals realize they've been duped. I'll make discreet enquiries with the HR Department at the University to check that this Makin fellow is not an ex-member of staff. Meanwhile, I'd be grateful if you would assist our artist in making up a composite of the man's face; it'll be most helpful when we make enquiries this afternoon in the road where he took delivery of the package."

He looked at Stephen as he got up to take Jo to a room down the corridor. "You may like to come with her and see how it's done: quite fascinating!" he said.

Before he had time to open the door, a constable appeared to say that there was no record of a John C Kelly having been a professor at Oxford at any time during the last thirty years.

"Fakes all round!" the detective muttered before glancing at Jo. "It looks as if your old boss must also be up to no good!"
......

When the police artist took them back to the detective's office with several copies of his computerized artwork, the young man gave them a broad smile that widened even further when he saw the quality of the picture Jo had helped to produce.

"Excellent!" he exclaimed. "Sit down for a few minutes and drink the tea I've just had delivered." He was obviously pleased about something and gave them a brief rundown.

"We're already making good progress. First, I've an appointment in half an hour with the woman who lives in Number 26. Secondly, I've been in contact with a helpful detective sergeant at Thames Valley HQ in Kidlington, just north of Oxford. He's had the bright idea of asking computer experts at the Culham Centre for Fusion Research and the Atomic Energy Research Establishment at Harwell to examine the coding. Both are about fifteen miles south of Oxford and it's quite possible that it may have been stolen from one of them. Even if it's neither, their experts may have some ideas about its origin."

After he had made a note of their mobile numbers on his smartphone and Stephen had indicated roughly where they intended to go for the next few days, he stood up and shook them both by the hand. "Thanks for all your help."

As he was guiding them to the main entrance, it occurred to Stephen to ask where the No. 59 bus stopped and how frequently it ran in the Callander direction.

The detective grinned happily as he informed them that his girlfriend commuted on the 59 bus from a nearby village. "I'll give her a quick call," he said, moving over to a quiet corner of the foyer.

Within two minutes he returned. "They leave three minutes before every hour and so the next one is at 11:57. If you walk quickly you'll easily make it. Have a good hike!"

Twenty minutes later, Jo and Stephen clambered aboard the waiting bus and found a seat. After all the rather frenetic activity of the last 24 hours, it was only when the bus moved off that they really appreciated the fact that their walking holiday was about to start.

Stephen looked at Jo sitting beside him. She seemed to be blossoming before his eyes as all the worry about the curious affair she had unwittingly got caught up in fell away.

She noticed his gaze and their eyes met for a moment in shared anticipation of their new-found freedom and the hiking to come.

A mere twenty minutes later, the bus stopped outside the entrance to Blair Drummond Safari Park and several people got off.

Chapter 6: The Trossacks

Jo looked at Stephen, wondering why he had made no move to leave the bus.

He shook his head. "We need the next stop," he explained. "According to my map, the A873 going east to Aberfoyle is nearly half a mile further on the left. We must keep our eyes peeled!"

The bus pulled in for the second time and they alighted. Jo looked around in surprise. "Where's the village? The only building I can see near this road is that church in the distance."

"I suspect Blair Drummond is basically the Safari Park and a few scattered farm buildings, although the map also marks a primary school," Stephen replied. "I was hoping to find a café for a quick snack and cold drink, but we may have to make do with water until we get a bit further along the A873. It'll waste too much time to go back to the Safari Park and we've got 14 miles to cover!"

Jo laughed. "I'll tighten my belt! It's a good job the breakfast was so substantial."

"Anyway, it's only 12:28 and the village of Thornhill is about five miles away; I expect there's a pub or something there," he replied hopefully.

"Two fit people like us should easily be able to get there well before two o'clock, especially on this straight flat road," she grinned, giving him a challenging look. "See if you can keep up with me!"

She strode off effortlessly at a good pace and he followed with a chuckle. "You lead, I'll follow. It would be safer to keep in single file, although I must say this road has much less traffic than the A84."

It was also slightly narrower and crossed an attractive landscape of fields dotted with occasional farm buildings; quite delightful under the bright midday sun in an almost cloudless sky. Stephen could tell that Jo was enjoying this sense of freedom on the open road. He certainly was and her presence made it so much better.

......

In the centre of the village, they saw the welcome sight of a white building with a sign announcing the "Lion and Unicorn Hotel".

Jo hesitated for a moment, concerned that it might be rather expensive, but Stephen ushered her inside.

"This is my treat," he whispered. "We need a decent short break and a clean loo!"

In fact the place turned out to be an excellent choice. They had a light bar meal with a cold drink followed by a nice cup of coffee in pleasant surroundings, so much so that they were almost sorry when it was time to move on.

The beautiful landscape continued until the road joined the A81 winding its way south from Callander to Glasgow. Now on a busier route for the next few miles, the walkers had to exercise more care, but, with Jo setting the pace again, it was not long before they came to a small roundabout to the southeast of Aberfoyle and bore right on to the A821 through the village.

It was just after five o'clock. Although they had only had a few mouthfuls of water since the last stop, they agreed that it was more important to find accommodation: Aberfoyle was clearly a popular tourist spot even in June.

"The place must be really crowded in late July and August!" Jo remarked, just as her companion spotted the Visitor Information Centre.

"They should have information about accommodation in there," he said.

To their relief, a member of staff told them that she had just received a telephone call from a small guesthouse with only two bedrooms to say that a twin room had been cancelled an hour earlier and asking her to mention it to anyone making an enquiry.

"The guesthouse is on the edge of the village a short distance up Duke's Pass on the A821," the young woman said. "The woman there occasionally 'phones us because she suspects that people looking for accommodation sometimes see the open country and turn back into the village again before seeing her house. The two rooms share a bathroom with separate bath and walk-in shower."

"We'll go there straight away," Stephen said and went on to express his thanks for her help so gratefully that the woman smiled and offered to 'phone ahead to say they were coming.

As the young couple walked on through the village and up the slight gradient, Stephen said: "We'll be going this way tomorrow morning and so can simply carry on up the hill."

After several bends in the road, they came to the edge of the village and spotted their objective tucked away down a turning. It had a modest sign beside the gate. "It really needs one on the main road," Jo said.

"Probably too expensive and it may be difficult to get permission. It doesn't help having only one off-road parking space."

"Trust a man to notice that!" she replied.

The elderly woman who answered the door looked relieved to see them. After Stephen had signed the visitor's book, she led them upstairs to a small but pleasant room.

"The family of three in the large double-bedded room is not coming back until after seven o'clock and so you might like to take the opportunity to have a shower before that," she said. "I'd be grateful if you don't use the bath because the hot water system will have a struggle to keep up! The little lad usually has a bath in the evening."

"We always have showers," Jo said. "The room is lovely; we're so glad you had a vacancy."

"I'm glad you like it. Now, what time would you like breakfast?" the woman asked.

"About 7:15 if possible," Stephen said, "We need to start walking in good time."

"That can be arranged. My husband cooks the breakfast now that he's retired, which is a great help."

There were no facilities for making a hot drink and so the young couple had to make do with yet more water. Nevertheless,

31

much refreshed by a good shower, they set out on the short walk back into the centre of the village just before seven o'clock.

It now seemed quite natural for Jo to link arms with her companion. Looking at her with pleasure, Stephen was delighted that she felt as comfortable with him as he did with her.

She looked up at him with a cheeky grin. "I'm paying for the meal tonight and don't you dare argue with me!"

The restaurants and cafés still open in the evening were quite busy, but they managed to find one with a reasonably priced menu displayed outside and had a good meal after some delay.

While they were waiting for the food, Stephen produced his map and showed Jo their route for the first leg of the following day's walk.

"First, we go north on the A821 as it winds up Duke's Pass, climbing 200m in about two miles. After slowly descending for another couple of miles, I suggest we turn off along a track that goes along the southern shore of Loch Achray and then north again to rejoin the A821 at a village called Brig o'Turk. This saves us at least a mile because the A821 has to loop round the western end of Loch Achray before it can go east to join the A84 just north of Callander."

He pointed to the places he was naming and traced the line of the short-cut with his finger.

"I'm really looking forward to tomorrow," Jo responded enthusiastically.

Stephen indicated a brief note he had made on a sheet of paper listing some useful information for the hike: "Brig o'Turk Tea Room, 5 miles west of Callander – good food and coffee".

"I know this is only about six miles out of Aberfoyle," he said, "but it's another 15 miles before we can get a late meal in Mhor, just off the A84, and so it might be sensible to have a brief coffee stop. Then we carry on along the A821 until just before the A84 junction. The map shows a path that goes north roughly parallel to the main road but separated from it by a small river. Are you happy to cover a total of 21 miles before having something to eat?"

"Of course I am!" Jo retorted. "We'll have had a good breakfast."

......

They set out at 8:15 on a sunny Saturday morning. "We've been lucky with the weather so far!" Jo murmured as she strode north up the road towards Duke's Pass. It was quiet at this time of day and Stephen risked walking alongside her, except when nearing one of the many bends in the narrow road.

"There'll be beautiful views soon," he promised, "Once over the Pass, we may even be able to glimpse Loch Achray in the next valley."

Jo gave a big sigh of pleasure. "It's beautiful already! Thank you so much for bringing me this way and for planning the whole route towards Mallaig; on my own I'd have been wandering around aimlessly still carrying my worries."

He looked at her. Her face was a pleasure to behold; all her cares seemed to have fallen away and she was even more relaxed than on the previous afternoon.

Although they did not manage to see Loch Achray until they were close to it, the gradual descent from the Pass was delightful, the distant broad sweep of sunlit mountains providing a splendid backdrop to complete the scene.

"You promised me beauty and you've certainly delivered on that promise!" Jo exclaimed in delight at one point.

To Stephen, however, her pleasure was much better than any view. "I really must be falling in love," he thought as happiness welled up within him. "Her feelings and thoughts are now more important to me than my own!"

Jo was almost disappointed when they eventually turned off the attractive road and he guided her down a track on the right. Very soon, however, she was rewarded when they reached the south bank of the Loch and walked within 50 yards or so of the water for about half a mile. There was no need to keep an eye out for passing traffic and the view over the tranquil water to the northern bank exuded a sense of peace. The whole delightful scene was frame by the mountains she had so appreciated when viewed from the higher ground.

Leaving the water's edge, the path meandered on for another half mile before they entered a well-maintained track and passed a pub – still closed – before emerging on the A821 just west of Brig o'Turk.

The Tea Room turned out to be housed in a single-storey wooden building painted dark green. Inside, however, the plain varnished walls and ceiling gave newcomers a comfortable friendly welcome.

"If the coffee tastes as nice as it smells, we're in for a treat," Jo thought, as Stephen gave their order to the smiling girl in charge. The place had only just opened and delicious-looking cakes were being brought out of the kitchen.

"I'm sorry it's still too close to breakfast to be hungry yet, even after six miles of fast walking!" she said.

......

Leaving the village, the road passed through a wooded area of more mature trees than they had seen on the higher ground. Brief views of Loch Venacher appeared quite frequently through the vegetation before they emerged into much more open country that became increasingly pastoral on the approach to Callander.

It was only when Jo spied a stone bridge not far ahead that Stephen pointed to a metal-barred gate on the left.

"I think this is the entrance to the path that runs up towards Mhor; it's almost alongside the river," he said.

The valley of the little river "Garbh Uisge" was just as beautiful as the landscape already encountered. A densely wooded ridge lay on the far side of the narrow waterway and A84 trunk road; in contrast, on their side of the river, the ground rose steeply up the flanks of a series of low mountains.

"Our side of the river is better and walking on a path is more enjoyable than using the road," Jo said appreciatively.

The next eight miles passed surprisingly quickly at the smart pace she was setting and Stephen only looked at his map again when the path widened to a well-maintained track, quickly followed by a narrow lane.

"We're just approaching the village of Strathyre on the A84. In view of the time, I suggest we turn off here and join the road for the short distance remaining to Mhor," he said. "If we stick to our present route it'll take a detour before swinging back to the road."

They took a right turn down a narrow path and across a pedestrian footbridge over the river to the busy road. Although they immediately passed a pub, Jo was happy to go a little further encouraged by the prospect of good food to come.

In the end, they almost missed Mhor because the road crossed the tiny hamlet on a bridge and it was necessary to swing right off the carriageway and drop down on to a lane that ran past the hotel.

Although almost two o'clock in the afternoon, they managed to order a cold salmon salad accompanied by a long cool drink. While they were waiting for the food, Stephen happened to pass the reception desk on his way back from the cloakroom and spotted a leaflet showing several local walking and cycling routes. Looking at it a few moments later with Jo, he was pleased to see that it contained much more detail than his Ordinance Survey map.

"Look!" he said. "It shows a walking route that passes just west of Lochearnhead and goes north up Glenogle, roughly parallel to the main road, before branching north-east to Killin at the western end of Loch Tay. It's only ten miles. If you can manage it, I could try to book accommodation in Killin using my notebook, assuming this hotel has a broadband connection. Glenogle should be splendid on a fine day like this. The leaflet says the Falls of Dochart in Killin are a "must see" as well!"

"You've certainly sold the walk to me!" Jo declared. "We should be able to cover ten miles in under three hours, unless the path is really steep!"

After getting permission to use the hotel's Wi-Fi, Stephen returned to their table and connected his notebook. He quickly showed Jo a view of the Falls of Dochart to whet her appetite before consulting Google Maps for possible lodging places.

As soon as they finished eating their light but nourishing meal, he made some calls on his mobile. It was second time lucky and he managed to reserve a twin room for the night in a modest B and B a short distance beyond the Falls.

As they left the hotel, Jo slipped two £20 notes into Stephen's hand. "But your share of our accommodation is not as much as this!" he objected.

"You've paid for the coffee and lunch today," she retorted.

"Then tonight's meal is also on me!" he insisted, as he reluctantly accepted the money.

"We'll see how much it is," she warned.

They followed the directions in the leaflet and walked under the A84 before turning right on to a path that ran parallel to the road in the direction of Lochearnhead. After many twists and turns, they found themselves on a delightful route running northwest up the side of a valley between beautiful ridges clad with a mixture of small bushes, bracken and heather.

"This is Glenogle and the stream not far below us is Ogle Burn," Stephen announced.

Jo took a deep breath of the delicious air. "You were certainly right about the place being beautiful: the best scenery so far!" she said delightedly.

From time to time they caught sight of the main road on the far side of the burn. "That's the A85 now: it took over from the A84 at Lockearnhead, having come in along the northern side of Loch Earn," he informed her, adding, as the path gradually dropped down towards the road and a lay-by, "We cross over here."

"I'm so glad we don't have to walk along this!" Jo exclaimed when she saw the traffic. "I suppose there are a lot of day-trippers about on a Saturday afternoon."

Soon the path climbed away from the road again and followed numerous twists and turns before dropping down to a much narrower road than before.

"This is the A827 and we've arrived on the edge of Killin and the River Dochart," Stephen said, pointing to a rapidly flowing river on the far side of the road. "You're in for a treat in about two hundred yards!"

Chapter 7: The Falls of Dochart

Stephen guided Jo a short distance up the road through Killin. The turbulent river was surging past and she enthusiastically crossed the road to stand beside a low stone wall on the river's edge. He joined her and stood protectively between her and the oncoming traffic before encouraging her back on to the pavement so that they could press on to the point where the road turned sharp left to cross a stone bridge.

The young couple's first direct view of the Falls of Dochart was therefore upstream towards the end of Loch Tay. Even though Jo had seen a picture on the small screen of Stephen's notebook, she was not prepared for the scene that greeted her eyes; the water rushed towards them past a series of large flat rocks on one side of the river before surging below them under the bridge.

"This is what I call a river!" she announced. "I could gaze at this for ages! Can we come back later after we've found our guesthouse and had a meal?"

"Of course we can," Stephen retorted, pleased at her reaction. "Let's just cross over now and look downstream."

As soon as they did so, her delight increased still further. The river had widened considerably to embrace a small tree-covered island and created a broad basin just downstream of the bridge where writhing water battled its way past large lumps of rock determined to impede its passage. On either side of the island, the escaping water merrily pursued its intention of reaching some unknown destination with all possible speed.

Jo walked on up the road beside her companion almost bubbling over with the thought of spending the evening and night in such a beautiful place and she was even more pleased when the twin-bedded room booked a few hours earlier turned out to have a small shower room.

Her enthusiasm continued as they walked back down the street in search of a restaurant an hour later.

"It was good to have an en-suite bedroom for the price charged," Stephen said. "Although it has the tiniest shower I've ever seen!"

"Probably made for caravans," she agreed, linking arms without a second thought.

......

They enjoyed an excellent meal of Loch Tay pan-fried brown trout fillets and vegetables, followed by strawberries and ice cream, in a modest little restaurant that filled up rapidly soon after their quite early arrival.

"You made a good choice, judging by the delicious meal we've just had and the place's obvious popularity," Jo said contentedly. "Quite a lot of the folk in there appeared to be local: always a good sign."

Stephen had been surprised but happy that she had left it entirely up to him to make the choice of where to eat. It was another sign that she was getting increasingly comfortable in his company. All he knew was that he loved every minute spent with her.

After they had strolled down to the Falls again and soaked in the views, Jo said she was still full of energy and asked if they could walk to the bank of the Loch.

"I'd love to, if you're happy to do a round trip of two miles," was the reply, and so it was a contented couple who set out arm in arm back past their guesthouse in what Stephen believed to be the right direction.

It was fortunate that he stopped to ask a local man the shortest way to the end of the Loch because they were directed to a narrow path that crossed the River Lochay on a pedestrian footbridge and cut a substantial corner off the road route.

"The Lochay is the twin of the Dochart and also takes its water from the 15-mile long Tay," the man explained proudly as he finished giving them directions.

It was not long before they were standing looking out over the placid water that stretched out before them as far as the eye could see in the gathering dusk. Stephen felt so moved to be standing close to Jo that he cautiously put his arm around her slim waist. She looked up at him with a shy smile. Very slowly their lips came together in a brief kiss before they turned to look out over the water again.

"Today has been one of the happiest days of my life," her soft voice said dreamily.

"I'm so glad; it's been exactly the same for me," he whispered.

Her face seemed to glow with happiness and they came together for another kiss before reluctantly turning to go back the way they had come.

"I'm sorry I didn't think to bring my small torch," he said.

"Never mind; we can still just see and it's not far to go. In fact, the darkness is all part of the magic!" she replied, giving his arm an excited squeeze.

......

They slept well that night and were up bright and early. After breakfast, Jo went upstairs to pack her rucksack while Stephen remained downstairs finishing a cup of tea. When he joined her in the bedroom, however, she was looking as white as a sheet.

"What's wrong?" he exclaimed.

"My boss has just 'phoned in a foul mood," she said. "His Oxford friend contacted him soon after seven o'clock this morning in a terrible state to say that Professor Makin has found several important pages missing from the book. He asked me if I had tampered with the PDF file. I replied truthfully that I had no idea how to do such a thing. I'm not sure if he believed me, but he merely asked where I was now. I foolishly panicked and told him I had spent the night in Killin. He was silent for a moment or two and then said he wanted me to start walking towards Crianlarich as soon as possible and that he would 'phone again when he had worked out what to do. With that he hung up before I had time to ask why."

Jo looked so worried and puzzled about the strange instruction she had been given that Stephen sat on the bed beside her and put his hand reassuringly on her knee.

"Don't worry! There's no harm in letting him know where you are. Prevaricating would only have aroused his suspicions further, but thank goodness you didn't mention me! What really puzzles me is why he wants you to walk towards Crianlarich; he can't possibly know that's the way we were planning to go. If he wanted you back in Pangbourne, he would have told you to aim for Stirling......Just a minute; I think Crianlarich is on the railway line between Fort William and Glasgow."

He unfolded his Ordinance Survey map. A moment later, he was pointing to the tiny symbol that marked Crianlarich station. "As soon as you're ready, we'll set out. I'll just look at my leaflet on local walks and cycling routes to see if there's any way of avoiding having to go all thirteen miles by main road."

Fortunately, he was partly successful; only ten minutes later they were following a lane that ran parallel to the A827 but on the northwest side of the River Dochart. The walking map indicated that it would take them about five miles before turning south to cross the river and join the busy A85 for the last eight miles to Crianlarich.

Even though the day was cloudy with very little sunshine, the little lane made walking a pleasure. They even managed to go over a mile before the first car passed.

The rapidly flowing river was a few yards away behind a fringe of trees. On the right, sheep grazed in wide fields that reached as far as the lower slopes of grass and bracken covered hills. Later the lane, now with frequent passing places, climbed gently for a short distance until they were able to look down over the river.

"This is a splendid route!" Jo exclaimed, seemingly having left her problems behind in Killin. "The view across the valley is lovely even on a rather dull day."

Stephen agreed, but he was privately puzzling about what course of action to take if her boss ordered her to return home. It would be sensible to pretend to obey because they must avoid giving him any hint that he was under discrete investigation by the police; at least he sincerely hoped that was the case. He was loath to spoil Jo's regained happiness by suggesting this subterfuge to her.

The narrow lane gradually descended through several peaceful copses before entering a larger wood and approaching the river again, until only separated from it by a ribbon of fairly dense foliage. Not far ahead, the lane bore sharp left to cross the water on a stone bridge.

A silver car was parked in a lay-by just beyond the bridge. A tall man stood beside the driver's open door, giving the appearance of having turned off the main road for a short break.

Jo grinned mischievously at her companion and took up the crouching pose of a sprinter. "Race you to the bridge!" she challenged. "The loser buys the drinks with our meal tonight!" With that she shot off.

Stephen, whose thoughts were still wandering, was slow to respond. She had almost reached a large tree on the right-hand side of the lane before he got going in earnest.

Everything then happened so quickly it was as if a film had been speeded up.

Chapter 8: Escape to Crianlarich

To Stephen's horror, a stocky man leapt out from behind the large tree and pinned Jo against its broad trunk.

"Take your hands off her!" Stephen bellowed.

Still holding Jo with one hand, the man turned and raised his fist. "Mind your own business or you'll be sorry!" he snarled.

"I'm not afraid of a cowardly bully like you!"

This so incensed the man that he let go of Jo completely and rushed at Stephen. The latter was no boxer but rowing had made him strong and he stood his ground, full of anger at the threat to the girl he loved.

Fortunately, the sound of a car engine roaring into life caused the burly man to falter, upon which a fist caught him a sharp blow on the chin followed by a second much harder punch in the centre of a sizable beer belly.

The man, doubling up in pain and temporarily winded, sank to his knees on the grass verge just as the silver car shot over the bridge and screeched to a halt on the other side of the tree with its bonnet a few feet from the trunk.

The driver jumped out with a vicious-looking truncheon in one hand and advanced threateningly on Stephen.

"Professor Makin! What on earth are you doing?" Jo cried.

"You've got something of mine. I'm going to get it out of you after I've dealt with your boyfriend!" was the very un-professorial retort as he surged forward.

Courageously, Jo stuck her foot out as he shot past. Her timing was perfect; he crashed to the ground with a sickening thud. Rather incongruously, the short truncheon rolled harmlessly forward until it came to rest at Stephen's feet.

He quickly picked it up and stepped over the professor's prostrate form to grab Jo's hand and urge her onward. "We'll go this way," he said, pulling her down a narrow path that left the outer corner of the lane's sharp bend and disappeared into the wood.

"I'll look at the map in a minute," he gasped. "At least we're still going in roughly the right direction and a car can't follow us."

They stopped and looked back just before the trees cut off their line of vision. The burly accomplice had crawled over to the professor's prostrate body and was trying to turn him over.

"I hope he's not dead!" Jo exclaimed in anguish as they began to run again.

"Don't worry; he's only been knocked out. If he needs medical attention and his accomplice can't drive, he'll have to flag down a passing car or 'phone for an ambulance...Come on, we must get to Crianlarich...'phone the detective in Stirling...to tell him...about Professor Makin...I should've noted the number...of that VW Passat!"

His words had begun to emerge in brief bursts as they pelted on and Jo replied in similar fashion: "You can't think of everything...I think you're...wonderfully brave...At least you have the...truncheon as evidence!"

After they'd run about a mile, Stephen slowed to a halt and searched in his wallet for the detective's business card.

"I'll probably have to leave a message; being Sunday, he may well be off duty," he said as he tapped the number into his 'phone and waited. "Drat, I think my signal strength is too weak. I'll try again nearer Crianlarich. If unsuccessful, we'll have to see if Crianlarich police station is open."

He gently pulled Jo round to face him and hugged her. "I'm so sorry to have let this happen to you," he whispered over her shoulder. "I should've realized that the real reason your boss 'phoned you was simply to make sure you kept your mobile switched on waiting for his next call. It has nothing to do with the fact that Crianlarich is on the railway line to Glasgow. The crooks must have an expensive smartphone with an "app" that enables them to use GPS to track you. The phony professor obviously managed to get fairly close yesterday but lost you when you turned your mobile off while we were having lunch."

"Why, yes!" Jo said. "I was trying to save the battery."

"The crooks must have assumed you were aiming for Crianlarich when they lost you yesterday. As it happens, of course, we turned in the opposite direction to Killin. Anyway, you must turn it off now and keep it off. Use my 'phone if you need one; it's a cheap one but works fairly well."

She hurriedly did as requested while he consulted the walking map.

"Apparently this path will eventually pass a farm and turn south over the river to join the A85 about two miles nearer Crianlarich. A note says that some of the path is not suitable for ordinary bicycles, only for mountain bikes and walkers with stout footgear. That's why the preferred route is to join the main road by staying on the lane."

They hurried on, eventually reaching the main road after many twists and turns and ups and downs.

"We must now keep our eyes peeled, although I very much doubt if those two are in any fit state to search for us!" Stephen said.

As they marched along in single file facing the oncoming traffic, Jo called over her shoulder: "I suppose the reason they didn't catch up with me earlier is that your trickery was only discovered yesterday."

"Yes, probably about midday. Once they'd got your 'phone number from your boss, the clever GPS app told them where you were and so they drove up from Stirling. The Professor must have been tracking us before we reached Mhor. He would've been hopping mad when you turned your 'phone off. I hope they had a really uncomfortable night waiting to get a signal again!"

......

Very fortunately, the small police station in Crianlarich was open; the door was unlocked by a young constable in shirt-sleeves when they rang the bell.

He grinned at them in a rather un-policeman-like way. "You're lucky this station is open today," he said, "It's my turn to be on duty until midday. How can I be of help?"

When Stephen told him what had nearly happened to Jo and that it involved a case of theft being investigated by a detective constable in Stirling and the Thames Valley police, the friendly man invited them in and insisted on providing cups of instant coffee.

"Unpleasant things like this can be a nasty shock," he said. "I'll put out an alert for a silver VW Passat while you drink it and then get in touch with this DC in Stirling. What did you say his name was?"

As Stephen handed him the detective's card, Jo suddenly blurted out: "SM59!"

The two men looked at her in astonishment.

"That's the first part of the car's registration number," she explained. "Stephen and I ran past the front of the car as we escaped. Somehow the initials SM have lodged in my mind because of their similarity to Professor S S Makin's fake name!"

"That's most helpful," the constable declared. "S indicates the car was registered in Scotland and M is one of the letters for the Edinburgh area. A silver VW Passat SM 59... narrows the hunt considerably. We should be able to find the registered owner fairly quickly."

He was even more surprised when Stephen fished the small truncheon, carefully wrapped in a plastic bag, out of his rucksack.

"I grabbed this as we escaped," he said. "Luckily I got hold of the business end, not the handle, and so there should be some of Makin's finger prints on the handle; he was gripping it really tight until he crashed to the ground. You're welcome to take a set of my prints so that they can be discounted."

The young man smiled approvingly as he left the room. It was not long before he returned. "I spoke to a sergeant in Stirling. He'll get a message through to your detective constable, who may ring you direct sometime tomorrow. I've said to use your number, Sir, not that of the young lady. Also, as you suggested, the sergeant would like me to take your finger prints; it's a quick process. He also wants me go to the spot where you were attacked in case there are any clues to pick up."

He looked rueful. "Bang goes the first part of my afternoon off! I'd be grateful if you could draw me a sketch of the layout: the position of the tree, where the car stopped and roughly where the man fell. I'm familiar with that little stone bridge fortunately."

......

After the surprisingly quick process of providing finger prints, the young couple were about to depart at 11:45 when the young constable asked where they were heading.

"Last night, I booked the one remaining room in a small guesthouse at the Bridge of Orchy," Stephen replied.

"You're in for a splendid walk, especially after you leave the village of Tyndrum, five miles up the A82. You can join the route of the Old Military Road that once went all the way to Fort William; parts of this have been incorporated into the West Highland Way. My girlfriend and I love that walk! To join the Way at its closest point to here involves quite a long detour. If you're worried about the time after this morning's delay, it would be quicker to go direct to Tyndrum and pick it up there."

He looked at his watch. "Public transport is very infrequent, especially on a Sunday, but the Oban train will come through here in ten minutes. Turn left as you leave here and then left again almost immediately; the train station is a four-minute walk at most. Ask for Tyndrum Lower: it's the first stop. A short walk will take you into the centre of the village where you'll find the excellent Real Food Café on the northbound side of the A82. After that you'll have plenty of time for a superb walk winding along the lower slopes of two mountains to the Bridge of Orchy, named after a stone bridge that crosses the River Orchy."

He unlocked the door and stepped outside with them. After shaking hands, he said: "Carry on up this road and turn first left for the station or continue on until you reach a roundabout and take the A82 to Tyndrum. Have a good holiday!"

Stephen thanked him for all his help and guided Jo left. "Let's take the train, have some refreshment in Tyndrum and then celebrate our freedom with a hike amongst the hills!"

Chapter 9: Bridge of Orchy

The short train journey to Tyndrum passed through a beautiful landscape that got even better as it progressed.

"We're in for a wonderful afternoon," Jo said, as she gazed out of the window. "And look, there's much more blue sky than earlier!"

Stephen smiled gently at her, enjoying her pleasure.

Thirteen minutes on the train and another four-minute walk saw them entering the Real Food Café. It turned to be just as good as the policeman had promised.

"Someone in the café told me that the West Highland Way leaves Tyndrum on the northern edge of the village," Stephen announced. "If we go up the other side of the A82, we'll come to a shop called the Mini-Market. The Way goes down a lane beside it."

They were striding up the narrow lane a few minutes later. After passing a small village hall, the tarmac gave way to gravel.

"This must be the Old Military Road that nice policeman mentioned," Jo said.

Very soon, she was surprised to see a major road appear on the left as the track came within a few feet of the verge.

"That's the A82 and we'll get close to it from time to time but it will always be to our left, whereas I think we cross the railway to Fort William several times," Stephen explained. "At the moment, it's somewhere over to our right."

"This track makes far better walking than having to squeeze along a narrow verge," Jo said, "and the scenery is getting better and better. The mountains look really beautiful, especially when shafts of sunlight strike their tops. Is it my imagination, or are they higher and more widely spaced than they were further south?"

"Definitely higher and approaching 1000m now," he replied. "They also look big because we're only at about 300m."

She was almost bouncing along in the belief that their troubles were over and everything was safely in the hands of the police.

Stephen delighted in her obvious happiness but had an uncomfortable feeling that Professor Makin and his associates still believed that she – or now he – had a copy of the uncorrupted material they wanted. He guessed that their industrial "mole" was unable to supply another copy and feared discovery now that the police had all the information. It was a possibility, therefore, that the "Professor" would attempt to waylay them again. Hopefully, his injury would keep him out of action for the next day or two at least. Without Jo's 'phone, it would be an extremely difficult task to track them down.

They had walked nearly a mile before the track crossed a small stream and the railway in quick succession and climbed gently to run along the grassy flank of a mountain, leaving the railway, stream and road a short distance below.

After another three quarters of a mile, the track appeared to be about to drop down towards the railway again when Stephen saw a small sign directing them on to a narrow path that climbed a little higher before levelling off. Jo looked up at the slope above their heads. Several crevices appeared to run down towards them.

"I suppose those lines are tiny streams making their way down from near the top," she said. "This is all so lovely. Do we have time to climb the slope?"

"We can easily spare an hour; it's less than five miles to Orchy now and we can still be there by five o'clock. However, we must be careful because we're only wearing stout trainers; proper boots would be better for such uneven ground."

They picked their way carefully up the steep slope. Well over halfway up, Jo turned to look at the view and held out her hand for Stephen to join her. She took a deep breath of the delightfully fresh air and murmured to herself: "What could be better than standing here feeling on top of the world and looking out over a splendid view holding hands with the man I love?"

Suddenly realizing she had spoken aloud, she went quite red in the face. "How embarrassing! The trouble is I feel so bubbly inside that the words just popped out!"

49

Her spontaneity both surprised and thrilled Stephen; her embarrassment made her even more irresistible.

"I'm so glad the words popped out," he exclaimed, "because I've been too shy to say that I think you're the most wonderful girl in the world. I can honestly say I had no idea what real love is until I met you, but now I'm head over heels in love with you!"

He swung her round to face him. Her arms went round his neck and they exchanged their first long kiss as he clasped her slim body. They remain like that for several minutes before she whispered: "I've not yet thanked you for bravely standing up to that thug and rescuing me; you really are my hero!"

"No one, absolutely no one, is going to hurt the girl I love and intend to marry – if she'll have me," he replied, overwhelmed by her kiss and his love for her.

Jo lifted her head from his chest, eyebrows raised. "Is that a proposal?"

Stephen squeezed her even tighter. "I know I'm not worthy of you, but I promise to love, honour and protect you for the rest of my life. In fact, I'm not sure if I can survive without you! I don't know how I have the nerve to ask…"

A finger pressed against his lips. "If you'll shut up for a minute, the answer is yes. Yes!!"

"You wonderful adorable girl!" He lifted her clear of the ground in his enthusiasm. "I'll do all in my power to make you happy and love you to bits!"

"Not completely to bits!" Jo laughed and then turned her head to look out across the valley again and shout, "I'm so happy!"

"How is all this possible in the space of precisely three days!" she exclaimed more quietly. "To think how I gave you the cold shoulder when you bumped into my table on the train."

"I didn't make a very good start, did I?" he grinned. "However, I think I began to fall for you when I saw a tear run down your cheek as you gazed out of the window."

"And there was I wishing you'd go away!"

"But we soon became friends!"

"Mainly because you were so clever at sorting out my problems."

"I was grateful to have such a good excuse to stay close."

"Well, I must admit I was slowly falling for your natural charm!"

This exchange helped them come back to some semblance of normality. They returned to the path and followed it down across the railway. For over one and a half miles the path ran alongside the stream until it merged with a larger stream. They crossed the latter on a sturdy bridge and joined more substantial track.

"This is definitely part of the Old Military Road again," Stephen said. "We're on our last three-mile stretch going slowly uphill."

The Old Road climbed to meet the railway and followed it closely all the way to Bridge of Orchy station. Here Stephen guided Jo down through the station underpass and into the tiny village.

"The guesthouse is just over there," he said, pointing to a cottage not far away.

A motherly woman welcomed them and led them down a short corridor. "We only have two rooms sharing a newly fitted bathroom with a walk-in shower. The couple in the larger room are staying for several days and using it as a base for touring. They've gone all the way to Oban today and won't be back until quite late, so there's plenty of hot water for you to have showers."

She opened the bathroom door to show them, clearly pleased with the recent renovation. She pointed to a large washbasin. "You may want to wash some smalls in here - it's larger than the one in the bedroom. You're welcome to hang your washing out to dry on a rack in our utility room; just knock on the kitchen door and I'll take you through."

Showing them into the bedroom she said apologetically: "When you spoke to my husband yesterday, I hope he warned you that the room is rather cramped and the beds are six inches narrower than a normal single bed; fine for teenagers but not so good for adults."

"Don't worry, we were glad to find anywhere at such short notice," Jo said kindly, noticing that Stephen was rather disconcerted to see that the narrow beds were pushed together in the centre of the room to allow space for a really small dressing table near the window. Beside it, a row of hooks on the wall was the only place for coats and other long garments.

The kindly woman looked relieved at her words. "I expect you'll be going to the hotel on the main road for something to eat later," she said, "but I'd be pleased to bring you both a cup of tea now. Do you take milk and sugar?"

They gratefully accepted tea with milk only and she disappeared.

Stephen looked at Jo apologetically. "I had no idea the beds would be crammed together like this. I really don't want you to get the wrong idea! I promise to keep my arms and legs under control and not intrude on your space. I love and respect you so deeply that I want our wedding night to be really special and......Oh help, I'm being so clumsy...."

Jo reached up and kissed his check. "I understand completely and feel honoured you think of me like that. I trust you absolutely!"

He was just about to hug her with relief when there was a knock on the door; the tea had arrived. Jo opened the door and expressed their thanks again as she took the small tray with its two mugs of hot tea.

"I'll bring these back when I come to the kitchen in about an hour's time with our small amount of wet washing," she promised.
......

The young couple strolled down the short lane to the Bridge of Orchy Hotel for their celebration dinner a few minutes before seven o'clock.

Jo was holding her companion's arm even more tightly than usual, almost as if she wanted to make sure he was not a dream and might suddenly disappear.

"I'm sorry I don't have any suitable clothes for the occasion," she said, looking down at the rather creased shirt and jeans she had worn on the journey to Stirling. At least, the weather was still dry enough to risk wearing some light sandals, although the overcast sky did not bode well for their long walk tomorrow.

"You look fantastic whatever you're wearing!" Stephen replied. "However, I wish I knew where to find an engagement ring for you – Fort William perhaps?"

Jo was silent for a moment and then lifted her right hand; she wore a silver ring with a small diamond set into the shank.

"I never knew my mother, but my grandparents brought me up until I was ten," she said softly. "Then my grandmother died and the social services thought my grandfather too old to look after me on his own and so I was placed with some foster parents living nearby. At least this meant I could keep in touch with my grandfather until he died three years later; then I was moved to a more permanent foster home on the outskirts of Pangbourne – the dear couple who have offered me temporary accommodation when I return from Scotland. The point of all this is that my grandfather left me my grandmother's engagement ring. It's the only personal connection I still have with my family. Would you be very hurt if I give it to you to place on my left hand?"

Stephen stopped and drew her round to face him. "That ring is very precious to you. You are very precious to me. It follows that the ring is also precious to me. I'd love you to wear it as a really meaningful engagement ring! We'll do the swap standing on the bridge over the River Orchy after dinner."

"I love you so much...," Jo whispered as they exchanged a kiss to seal the agreement.

They suddenly realized that they were now standing beside the A82 in full view of the large white hotel on the opposite side.

"I don't care who has seen us! I want to shout about my wonderful fiancée to the whole world!" Stephen exclaimed, as they crossed the road.

He paused at the reception desk to book a table for dinner and said that they would have a drink in the bar first. Jo only wanted an orange squash and so he bought two before joining her with the menus, the smaller one being the fixed-price two or three-course meal that was available until eight o'clock.

"Please choose something from the larger menu if you see anything you'd really like," Stephen whispered, but Jo set it firmly aside when she saw the prices. "The choice on the small one looks lovely," she insisted.

A waiter had come into the bar to take the dinner orders from several people. Being hungry, the young couple selected the soup of the day – potato, leek and butterbean – followed by sirloin steak with fresh vegetables.

In the restaurant, Stephen's eyes were only for his companion; she positively bubbled with happiness as she had done earlier in the day. He also realized that the experience of eating in a nice hotel was as novel for her as it was for him.

"I wish I could have afforded to get a bedroom here," he said at one point.

"We're fine where we are," Jo replied sensibly. "Our room has a lovely view and is very quiet. Just think what it might be like to have a bedroom at the front of this building; I don't suppose the traffic dies down until after midnight."

She insisted on keeping the cost down by only having a two-course meal, but they were comfortably full without a desert and finished with coffee at a table in a fairly quiet corner of the bar.

Stephen took out his little diary. "We need to plan our stopping points for the next few days," he said. "Before I came away, I printed off some details about the route of the West Highland Way from here to Fort William, after which most of the rest of the journey to Mallaig has to be on the road. Tomorrow night, we'll have a stop-over in Kinlochleven after a walk of about 21 miles. Then, on Tuesday, we cross the mountains to Fort William and continue on to somewhere near Glenfinnan. That leaves a fairly easy journey to Mallaig on Wednesday where I suggest we stay for two nights and take a trip to Skye by boat; it's only a half-hour crossing. As soon as I find a good Wi-Fi connection tomorrow, I'll search for a guesthouse near Mallaig for Wednesday and Thursday nights."

"A trip on a boat; how lovely!" Jo exclaimed. "Sorry, do go on."

"On Friday, we can return to Fort William on an early morning train; it's said to be a really beautiful journey. After that, we've got four more nights before we need to be in Glasgow on Tuesday week. I've already got my ticket to London on the train leaving just after midday; I'll book one for you on the same train."

......

Soon after, Stephen took Jo down a small road beside the hotel and she saw the river a short distance ahead. "This is where the West Highland Way starts again," he said as he led her on to a grey-stone bridge over the rapidly flowing water.

He put his arm around her shoulder as they gazed first downstream, where Jo spotted what she thought was one of the mountains they had passed during the afternoon, and then upstream in the direction they would be going tomorrow.

But there was important business to attend to and he took her right hand and very carefully twisted the little silver band off her finger. Then he took her left hand and held it.

"This little ring is already yours but I now place it on your engagement finger in token of the fact that I now belong to you and will love you always. Welcome to your new family!"

He gently pushed the ring on her finger and remained holding her hand while he hugged her to him with his other arm. Jo was too moved to speak but the kiss she gave him said far more than words.

Some time passed before they walked dreamily back to the guesthouse and got ready for bed. In the darkness, as they kissed goodnight, Jo said: "I think I mentioned how happy I was last night, but today has surpassed everything."

"For me too," Stephen said as he gave her hand a squeeze. He made sure that her thin duvet was in the right position before adjusting his own. His bed was so narrow that he realized he would have to take great care turning over during the night.

In fact, they both slept very well to start with, but, in the middle of the night, Stephen heard Jo tossing about and mumbling. Then her hand shot out and caught him in the chest.

"Are you all right?" he whispered.

Jo roused at the sound of his voice. "I'm so sorry; I was having a nightmare. I was walking along a road when that horrible thug sprang out from behind some bushes and dragged me towards a huge dark hole beside the road. I was struggling but he was much too strong for me."

Stephen reached out to grip her hand; he could feel her trembling. "You're completely safe with me," he whispered. "I love you and will guard you. In fact, you're my life from now on and your happiness is my top priority."

His words and touch were so loving and gentle that Jo could almost literally feel the fear gripping her being driven out by something far greater and more wonderful.

"I feel I've come home," she murmured as sleep began to overtake her again.

Still keeping hold of her hand, Stephen used his other arm to make sure that she was properly covered by her duvet before he carefully rolled on to his back again and gazed silently up at the ceiling. To his surprise, the first faint glimmer of dawn was penetrating the gap at the top of the curtains.

He could not help marvelling that, for the first time in his life and after several false starts at relationships, he had finally met a girl who completely bowled him over. It was not just that she was extremely attractive to look at but something far more important; she possessed what he could only describe as an inner beauty that reached out and held him captive.

"Jo really is my life and my hope," he murmured into the darkness as he drifted back to sleep.

Chapter 10: Surprised on Black Mount

Stephen's little alarm clock woke them at 6:45 on Monday morning. Jo drew the curtains and they saw that it had rained quite hard during the night; the nearby bushes were still dripping and there were occasional flurries of rain.

The young couple set out on the long hike promptly at 7:55 after a good breakfast. Although the sky had brightened slightly, spots of rain were still falling and they were wearing their lightweight waterproof anoraks and trousers.

"I'm glad we both had the sense to use plastic bags for our clothes because these waterproof covers only protect the top of the rucksacks!" Jo remarked. "We may run into almost horizontal rain if the wind gets up!"

Stephen grinned at her. "My trainers are supposed to be waterproof but that claim may be tested today!"

By this time they had crossed the bridge over the River Orchy to join the West Highland Way again. It was not long before the narrow track began to wind its way up over 100m to higher ground from which they were able to look down over a wide valley framed by a panorama of encircling mountains: beautiful even on a dull damp day.

"This is splendid now but would be fantastic on a sunny day," Jo said and laughed as a brief gust of wind flung a few raindrops in her face.

Stephen could not resist claiming one as he kissed the tip of her nose.

......

In complete harmony, they followed the winding route as it took them down for almost a mile towards a small group of white buildings.

"One of those is the Inveroran Hotel; it's on what must be an upgraded section of the Old Military Road," Stephen explained. "It's close to the southwestern corner of Loch Tulla. We'll be crossing several feeder streams before our route takes us northeast between the northern shore of the Loch and a beautiful group of mountains called the Black Mount. You'll be in for a treat, especially if the rain holds off!"

"I'm already enjoying a treat just walking with you, whatever the weather – at least within reason!" Jo said. She gave a little chuckle.

They joined a narrow lane and passed the attractive hotel. "I'm almost sorry it's too early for coffee," Stephen said.

"Some of the guests will still be having breakfast," she surmised.

It was not long before the lane ended at an isolated house – Forest Lodge according to a sign on the gate – and he guided her through another gate on to a gravelled track. The latter slowly climbed northeast for about three miles, skirting the edge of a conifer plantation before coming out on to a plateau 150m above Loch Tulla, now in the valley some distance to the south.

The views were impressive and they stopped to gaze in several directions; not far to the west towered the Black Mount group, some at almost 1000m, and, to the northwest, the even larger Glencoe cluster.

The expression on Jo's face delighted her companion, especially when she pointed due east: "I think I can see traffic passing on the A82; it must be well over a mile away!"

There was something rather homely about the sight of this tiny ribbon of road in this intensely lonely place, now under a leaden sky.

"I'm sorry we can't see all this on a sunny day!" Stephen said as they began to walk on.

"Never mind," Jo replied. "Even though we're quite likely to get caught in a downpour fairly soon, I'm still enjoying myself!"

They had encountered several walkers already this morning and another couple exchanged a friendly greeting as they passed on the way towards Bridge of Orchy.

"I must say most people we pass are very friendly," Jo commented. "It makes a pleasant change from the rather glum and preoccupied looks of folk in towns."

Directly ahead, the path crossed about half a mile of level ground and provided the opportunity to stride forward side by side at a good pace.

The only sound disturbing the silence was the faint scrunch of their footsteps, but suddenly they were startled by a man's voice close behind them.

"*I am* the way…the truth…and the life."

The words were crystal clear and somehow gentle and authoritative at the same time.

The young couple spun round in total astonishment. There was nobody in sight except for the walkers who had passed them a couple of minutes earlier and were at least two hundred yards away.

"Did you hear that?" Stephen gasped. "But where's the speaker? The nearest possible hiding place is at least 50 yards away!"

"The voice was definitely very close to us," Jo said, completely baffled.

She started walking around the area searching for clues. Strangely, she felt no fear; even the leaden sky seemed to be less threatening and there was a glimmer of something she could not define deep within her.

Stephen, on the other hand, was uneasy and it was not just because something completely out of the ordinary had occurred. When they walked on after discovering nothing unusual, he tried to analyze each phrase in turn; the most troubling one was the last, but the reason completely eluded him.

One and a half miles took them to a stone bridge over a narrow river. "This river feeds Loch Ba about two miles east of here," Stephen explained. He was almost desperately trying to restore some semblance of normality. "We've now got almost four miles to go before we cross the A82 and then less than a mile to the King's House Hotel and some refreshments. However, we've now got to climb another 150m or so."

When they reached the top of the ridge at a height of almost 500m, a vast expanse of valley opened up in the north. Appearing to be almost beside them, the peaks of Glencoe rose to an impressive height of over 1,100m, and, directly ahead, the A82 made its way in a wide arc towards the famous valley of Glen Coe.

Their rough path dropped gradually down and curved northeast around the northern slopes of the mountain to join a service road that carried visitors to and from Glencoe Activity Centre. Crossing the main road, they entered a narrow path that climbed very slowly again. There was now a splendid view of the entrance to Glen Coe: surprisingly wide and flat with high mountains on both sides.

"I don't know if it's just me but it looks rather forbidding!" Jo was obviously rather disappointed.

Stephen agreed but tried to be positive: "The sun would make all the difference."

They increased their pace, now quite anxious to get to their refreshment stop.

......

The King's House Hotel sat in an isolated spot but was clearly popular both with walkers on the West Highland Way and tourists who had made a short detour from the road, judging by the number of cars in the car park.

Nevertheless, the young couple enjoyed the chance to sit for a time with large cups of strong coffee waiting for their jacket potatoes to be prepared.

Stephen had managed to regain his normal composure and good humour following the remarkable earlier episode by putting his dilemma on what he liked to call his "back-burner". He even managed to avoid alarming Jo when a call came through to his mobile.

"It's only the Stirling detective," he whispered to her, carefully covering the mouthpiece with his thumb. The conversation lasted about three minutes during which time their piping-hot potatoes arrived overflowing with melted cheese and garnished with grated carrot and slices of tomato. It was fortunate that they were in a relatively quiet corner of the large room.

"That detective's a smart cookie," Stephen said when the call finished. "He's very sorry you were put through such an unpleasant experience, but it's turned out to be very helpful to them. There are some excellent prints on the truncheon handle and they've found the car; it was stolen in Stirling and then abandoned there but has yielded some useful clues. The computer code has been identified; we're not allowed to know the details but he reported that some people in high places are extremely grateful. Your old boss was arrested early this morning and is being questioned. Lastly, when we get to Fort William would we please go to the police station there and help make up a facial composite of the thug who attacked you. I said we'd be in Kinlochleven tonight and probably get to Fort William well before midday tomorrow, but that we wanted to move on towards Mallaig fairly quickly and so he's going to tell the station to expect us at 11:30 or soon after. Finally, he sends you his thanks and good wishes."

Leaving Jo to absorb this information, he tucked hungrily into his baked potato.

"I bet my estate agent's office is in chaos!" Jo said as she chewed some grated carrot.

Chapter 11: Kinlochleven

By twelve-forty, Jo and Stephen were walking west along the West Highland Way. The further they went, the more impressive the expanse of Glen Coe became, lined as it was on both sides by mountains that seemed to brood over the wide valley. The path ran parallel to the A82 for well over a mile before turning north to begin a steep climb up the adjacent slope.

"Now the real climb begins," Stephen announced. "You're in for a treat according the notes I printed off from the web. Take it carefully; we've plenty of time and should be in Kinlochleven by four o'clock."

A steep path paved with rough stone slabs made their passage up the initial slope relatively easy. It was not long before they crossed a bridge over a narrow gorge with a tumbling stream below them. The path first followed the stream but soon steepened and they found themselves zigzagging upwards until reaching some stone cairns that indicated the top of a wide pass between the adjacent peaks.

"This is the highest point on the West Highland Way at 550m," Stephen informed his slightly breathless companion. "We've climbed about 300m this afternoon, most of it within the last mile. Now we have a gradual descent for over four miles all the way down to sea level, Loch Leven being a sea loch."

"But I must look at the views first!" Jo exclaimed. "If only it was a nice day."

Stephen produced a small compass from his pocket and lined up due north. "Do you see the mountain directly north of us?" he asked. She nodded. "I think that's Binnein Mor: the highest one in that group at 1,130m."

There was a strong wind blowing from the north; in fact, for the first time that day, they were no longer too warm in their waterproofs. As Jo continued to look northward over the splendid but rather sombre array of mountains, she was surprised and delighted to see the clouds above Binnein Mor slowly part. It was like watching a slow action replay as some shafts of light struck the flanks of the mountain and it lit up as if in appreciation of the sun's caress.

......

The path descended slowly to a stream that had to be crossed on stepping stones before climbing again over a ridge and down to a bridge over a much larger stream.

Jo breathed in the slightly moist fresh air with pleasure as she moved on more rapidly down a winding path that soon deposited them on a track close to a building and a set of large grey pipes. She looked at Stephen enquiringly.

"We've joined a section of the Old Military Road again," he said. "I think these pipes are carrying water down to a hydro-power station that serves Kinlochleven."

The rough track gradually made its way downhill, past an attractive waterfall, and eventually crossed the River Leven before curving west to become a road that skirted the northern edge of Kinlochleven.

They had just passed a few scattered houses and a small housing estate when what they had been half expecting all day happened: heavy spots of rain fell and rapidly turned into a downpour.

Looking around for some form of shelter, the nearest building happened to be a small white church with a porch over its entrance. The young couple scampered down the short path and thankfully squeezed together under the modest shelter.

Trying to avoid rain that was not only being driven in by the wind but also bouncing off the pavement, Jo flattened herself against one of the double doors. To her surprise, it was not properly latched and opened slightly.

She looked at her companion. "Do you think it would be all right to go in and avoid getting splashed out here?"

"I suppose so," Stephen said. "Churches, especially rural ones, are often left open during the day and it's barely four o'clock."

They entered cautiously and were met by a loud whirring noise. An old woman was cleaning the carpet on a platform at the far end of the building. Becoming aware of their presence, she switched off the machine and came down the aisle to greet them with a smile of welcome on her weather-beaten face.

"Welcome to our little church! I'd like to think you've come to pray but I expect you're trying to escape the rain. I heard it drumming on the roof," she said, looking up rather anxiously as if fearing to see signs of water ingress. Although she spoke with a strong Scottish accent, her meaning was perfectly clear.

She looked at them again. "Come up to the front and sit down, or perhaps stand close to the electric heater I've just put on to warm my old bones while I have a cup of tea. The kettle's on in the vestry and I'll make some for you as well. You look cold as well as wet, poor dear!"

These last words were addressed to Jo, who did indeed look rather cold. The waterproofs she was wearing had managed to keep the water out but did not offer much thermal protection; the rain had been surprisingly cold.

"Thank you; we'd love a cup of tea," Jo said gratefully as they all moved forward to the front of the church and the old woman gestured towards an oil-filled electric heater that looked rather like a small version of an old-fashioned central heating radiator. It was already giving out some welcome warmth.

"You just make yourselves at home," the old woman said and disappeared through a nearby door. The young couple took off their rucksacks and stood on either side of the heater.

Jo found herself near an ancient wooden lectern. It was beautifully carved and she moved over to examine it more closely. A large Bible lay open on the sloping top. She looked down at the beautifully printed text and froze; shock mingled with a strange sensation of warmth left her speechless.

"Stephen, come and look at this!" she managed to whisper at last, pointing to the text.

The words that greeted his eyes left him stunned: "I am the way, the truth, and the life: no man cometh unto the Father, but by me."

At that moment the old woman appeared carrying a tray containing three mugs of steaming liquid. Glancing at the Bible as she passed, she said: "Ah yes, St John's Gospel, Chapter 14, was the New Testament reading yesterday. It's one of my favourite passages, especially in the old language of the King James' Bible. Being a Scot, I should call him King James the Sixth of Scotland, as he was before you folk pinched him in 1603 and made him James the First of England! Now sit down and have your tea before it gets cold."

Then she noticed that her visitors were looking extremely pale. "My dears, what's wrong? Come and sit here beside me and let me see if I can help."

"We'd better tell you what happened on our walk this morning," Jo said and started to recount the episode.

The old woman listened intently. As soon as Jo finished, she exclaimed: "You're amazingly privileged to have been spoken to by the Son of God! Jesus has never spoken audibly to me or my husband … before he died that is; it'll be different for him now of course!" A tear appeared on a weather-beaten cheek and Jo wanted to hug her.

The kindly woman brushed the tear away and continued: "The Bible says God's word never returns to him void. I take this to mean that God always speaks with the intention of achieving a result. He wants you to take notice and respond. If you feel totally inadequate, ask for his help."

She lapsed into silence while everyone sipped their tea. When she spoke again, however, the young people both experienced a strange sensation of warmth that was nothing to do with the hot liquid. They seemed to know instinctively that they were being offered something beyond their natural understanding.

"I find it helpful to think in terms of light and dark. Darkness cannot exist in the presence of light. All human beings are by birth and nature full of darkness to a greater or lesser extent; the Bible speaks of us as being "sinful" and it's so bad that we can't change ourselves even if we wanted to. In contrast, God is absolutely holy; in fact, his nature defines what true holiness is. It follows that we can never come into his presence either in this life or the next – after death that is – because our darkness cannot exist in the light of his holiness."

She then gave them a beaming smile as if to indicate that she was about to impart some good news.

"Because God loves us, he doesn't want to have to cut us off from his presence forever and so he came up with a solution. His Son, Jesus, who has existed for all eternity, was born as a baby to Mary 2000 years ago, lived a sinless life doing good, teaching and working miracles. He eventually went up to Jerusalem where he knew he would be arrested on a trumped-up charge and put to death by crucifixion. During that terrible time on the Cross, the Bible says that "God made Jesus who had no sin to be sin for us, so that in him we might become the righteousness of God". I still find this amazing truth hard to grasp, even after years of being a Christian, but it means that all who accept God's forgiveness can become "children of God". It's all possible because God is so loving and gracious. We certainly don't deserve it. All we deserve is God's judgement and condemnation!

"That's why Jesus has just let you know that he is the "way" to God; he is offering to become your new "life". Do take up his offer!"

Then Stephen became aware that she was looking directly at him. "If the person you long to live for is part of God's plan for you, that relationship will be wonderfully enhanced by his presence, provided only that he has first place in your life."

Normally, such direct words would have put Stephen's back up. This time, however, he felt something melting inside him and it was not just because such a gentle kindly old woman was the one speaking.

Jo had carefully looked down at her lap as soon as she realized the last few words were being directed at Stephen, but then felt the old woman's hand on her knee.

"I've just noticed your ring," the woman said softly. "I believe that explains why Jesus chose to speak to both of you at the same time. I'm certain your engagement is part of his plan for your life; so take heart, you can have a great future together."

Jo beamed at her. "Thank you for all your kindness, the tea and everything. Stephen and I need to start looking for tonight's accommodation. Do you know anywhere that's not too expensive? We need two beds but are happy to share a bedroom."

The old woman now surprised them even further. "I only have a small house, but there's a family room with three beds you're welcome to have for a very reasonable charge. I used to do B and B on a regular basis but not so much now that I'm getting older. There's a fairly good bathroom next door with a shower over the bath."

Then she looked dismayed. "Oh dear; I've just remembered I don't normally keep bacon in the 'fridge unless I know someone's coming. But there are plenty of eggs. I can do them in any form you like; my husband used to say I do the best scrambled eggs in the village - although I'm not sure how he knew!" She gave a little chuckle.

"Scrambled eggs are my favourite too!" Stephen asserted. He looked at Jo, who was nodding happily, before continuing: "We'd love to take up your kind offer."

"That's splendid!" the old woman said. "I'll just finish this carpet, wash up the mugs and take you down the road. I live very close by."

Jo insisted on washing up for her while she continued cleaning the carpet. Stephen walked slowly around the small church thinking about what they had seen and heard. He peered out of the door; thankfully the rain had almost stopped. Then he sat down at the back waiting for Jo and their hostess to join him.

As he gazed towards the front, he saw some words painted on the wall above the table on the platform. His attention was now so completely focused on the text he was hardly conscious that the old woman had switched off her vacuum cleaner and was carefully winding up the flex.

"Behold, I stand at the door and knock:" the words stated, "if any man hear my voice and open the door, I will come in to him, and will sup with him, and he with me." (Rev. 3:20)

Stephen had no idea what Rev. 3:20 meant, but he presumed it was referring to somewhere in the Bible. He was absolutely sure, however, that it was Jesus speaking.

"Come on Stephen!" Jo was holding out her hand to him invitingly. "Sarah is going to take us home."

Chapter 12: Over the Mountains

The rest of Jo and Stephen's time in Kinlochleven was very pleasant. Their new friend Sarah's house was small but homely and the three-bedded room comfortable, if a little cramped with so much furniture. Sarah had insisted on getting them what she called "a proper Scottish cuppa" before they had a shower, although Jo suspected that it was partly to give the water time to heat up.

Just as they were about to go out to find a meal, Sarah said: "I don't want to interfere with any plans you have, but my Fred used to enjoy an occasional half pint at the Tailrace Inn; it's less than half a mile away and the food is said to be good and reasonably priced."

"With a name like that, who could resist trying it?" Stephen said as they thanked her.

"What a dear old lady!" Jo said as they walked down the road. "I hope I'm like her when I get old."

"But I really would prefer to be with you and not die years before you like her husband," Stephen whispered.

"He was a forester and had a hard life," Jo replied. "Sarah told me they never had the money to eat a proper meal in a restaurant: only the very occasional drink and snack in a café or pub. If we stay here on our way back, do you think we could take her with us to the Tailrace – that is if it turns out to be as nice as she thinks?"

"Of course we can," Stephen said. "I've even got her telephone number so that I can book the accommodation in advance. It should be possible to space our daily journeys back to Glasgow and fit Kinlockleven into the timetable."

The Tailrace Inn did indeed serve excellent bar meals and they had an enjoyable evening together. It was almost inevitable, however, that their conversation mainly centred on the amazing things that had happened to them that day.

……

Because Stephen and Jo needed to get to the police station on the High Street in Fort William well before midday, Sarah provided breakfast at 7:15; her scrambled egg lived up to its reputation.

They waved goodbye to their kind hostess at eight o'clock and walked west along the northern edge of the village for about half a mile.

"Sarah refused to accept more than £30 for our accommodation," Stephen said. "I tried to persuade her to let me pay the going rate, but she said she was making a good profit at £30. She added that she wouldn't have had anyone last night if Jesus hadn't brought us into the church!"

"She really is a gem!" Jo said. "She seems to have such complete faith in God. It really is rather sweet! I was very moved by what she said last night but I still have difficulty fully believing it. However, we really must hang on to the fact that we both heard those words from St John's Gospel being spoken just behind us yesterday before seeing them in the open…"

She was interrupted by Stephen guiding her on to a path going north up a steep slope through a wood. It was quite rough and they had to take care of their footing.

"This path will carry on for about a mile until we rejoin the wider track of the Old Military Road and climb slowly northwest," he explained. "Then we'll stay on the Old Road all the way to Fort William instead of taking the West Highland Way semi-circular detour that goes via Glen Nevis. We can return that way when we have more time. The shorter route is about twelve and a half miles and so we should be able to get to the police station by 11:30."

They climbed steadily and crossed a narrow road. A little further on, the trees receded and the warmth of the sun on Jo's back prompted her to turn and to look back at the valley they had just left. In total contrast to the previous day, the scene was bathed in bright light. Even the mountains that framed the valley looked friendly and no longer slightly threatening.

"Isn't it splendid!" she exclaimed, smiling at Stephen as if inviting him to share her pleasure.

"It certainly is!" he replied as he took her hand and looked at her adoringly.

"She really is lovely," he thought. She was indeed; clad only in shorts and T-shirt, her slightly bronzed face, arms and legs almost seemed to glow with health and vitality.

They walked on and soon the path deposited them on the wider but very stony track of the westbound Old Military Road that proceeded to climb slowly for over two miles to the top of the pass at about 330m. The scenery got better and better as they progressed, especially when they began the gentle descent. The track wound its way along a wide valley with beautiful mountains on both sides and in the far distance.

"Thank you for bringing me to such a wonderful place!" Jo said at one point.

"It's far better sharing it with you!" Stephen replied. "Even the trek yesterday in the relative gloom was bright because of you!"

"I'm so glad," was all she was able to whisper.

By this time the track had gradually curved northwards and they continued the gradual descent, soon passing the point at which the narrow path of the West Highland Way left them on its way northeast towards Glen Nevis.

"I think Fort William is about four miles now," Stephen said.

It was not long before the rough track joined a narrow road that continued to descend until it crossed a stream and the scene became really pastoral with sheep grazing peacefully in fields on both sides. The outskirts of Fort William were visible some distance below with Loch Linnhe beyond. Half a mile later, they crossed a cattle grid and entered a residential road.

......

It took a further walk of three quarters of a mile before Jo and Stephen were halfway up the High Street outside an impressively large central police station. For some reason, Jo felt a slight shiver as they entered and walked up to the reception desk; she was certainly glad she had a reliable companion with her.

To their surprise, they were immediately taken up to the office of a chief inspector. "I thought we were just going to help with a facial composite," Stephen said to himself.

A man in smart uniform stood up as they were shown in and politely shook hands, the young couple feeling completely out of place in their walking gear.

"Put your rucksacks by the door and come and sit down. I expect you'd like some tea or coffee," he said before giving the order to the young constable who had brought them upstairs.

The man sat down behind his desk again and fiddled with some papers. "I have an apology to make to the young lady," he said. "You probably don't know it but for several hours yesterday afternoon and evening there was a warrant out for your arrest!"

Chapter 13: Mystery Explained

Jo looked at the chief inspector in total disbelief. "What crime am I supposed to have committed?" she gasped.

"None as it turns out. The Thames Valley people messed up by not keeping Stirling informed after the arrest of your boss early yesterday morning. When questioned, he tried to plead total ignorance of the theft and put the blame on you. He craftily suggested that they take a look at your bank account. When they finally did so, they found that £1000 in cash had been paid into it last Friday morning in addition to your normal month's salary."

By now poor Jo was so shocked that Stephen reached out to take her hand. "I'm sure there's been some mistake," he declared.

The inspector smiled. "Guess which branch of your bank was used and at what time," he said.

Jo shook her head despairingly. "I've no idea!" she muttered.

"It was in the Stirling branch at 10:53 last Friday!"

"Then I couldn't have done it! We arrived at Stirling police station soon after ten o'clock and were there for about an hour and a half. A very helpful detective constable interviewed us and I spent time with a police artist making up a facial composite of the so-called Professor Makin!" Jo began to breath more normally again.

"It's very lucky you were there! As soon as that alert DC heard about the warrant, he was able to persuade his superintendent to get on to Thames Valley and tell them to rescind it immediately," the inspector said. "Clearly, the crooks were trying to incriminate you by making it appear that you'd received the money in exchange for the stolen file on Thursday night."

Something that had long puzzled Stephen now became clear.

"Now I understand why Jo's boss told her to stay in Scotland for a whole week after making the delivery!" he said. "It was part of setting her up as a potential scapegoat to protect him if anything went wrong."

"As it turned out, that was what made Stephen suspicious and examine the SD card on his little laptop and find the computer code buried in the middle of a maths textbook," Jo explained.

"The silly thing is that if they'd used a high-powered book on physics as the hiding pace, I wouldn't have bothered to scan through it so carefully. Being careless and using an undergraduate mathematics text made me examine it further," Stephen added.

"But only because you're a mathematician and so recognized it," Jo reminded him. "An ignoramus like me wouldn't have known the difference."

"So, all in all, the criminals were out of luck!" the inspector summed up. "First, because you two met on the train; secondly, because the young man here is a mathematician and had the ability to corrupt the file; thirdly, because you reported to us as soon as you were sure a crime had been committed, and, finally, because they happened to pay the money in when you couldn't possibly have done it!"

Stephen, however, had not been paying full attention; something important had occurred to him.

"There are three main players here," he said. "The fake Oxford professor is probably the "mole" who managed to copy some pages from a confidential report. The so-called Professor Makin at this end is probably a senior member of a gang with the task of transferring the goods, possibly abroad, to the customer and making sure payment is made. That leaves Jo's boss. I'm beginning to suspect he's more important than he appears. He may well be the mastermind behind this theft and possibly others. That could be the reason he's prepared to spend substantial money protecting himself by setting Jo up as a potential scapegoat!"

"That's a possibility," the inspector said. "I'll pass it on to our smart DC in Stirling and get him to suggest to Thames Valley that they put the screws on that estate agent - using the correct procedure, of course!" he added hastily with a grin.

"Now, if you've finished your coffee, I'll get somebody to take you down to the police artist."

......

Stephen and Jo were rather longer in the police station than they had expected and did not reach the town pier until 12:20 seeking to find out the times of the ferry across the narrow straits between Loch Linnhe and Loch Eil.

"The small guesthouse I've booked for tonight is close to Glenfinnan, about 14 miles from here, but it will be more comfortable walking along the south side of Loch Eil on the A861 and only join the busier northern route on the A830 just before Glenfinnan," he explained.

The next ferry was due in 45 minutes. About to return to the town centre to find somewhere for a quick snack, they noticed a small seafood restaurant. "Time's short; let's try in here," Jo suggested.

They made sure that the food would come quickly by selecting the "dish of the day". It turned out to be a white fish they had never heard of, but the sauce was tasty and the chips just right.

......

A mere ten minutes on the water saw them disembarking with a number of other passenger on a jetty that made the modest town pier look enormous.

The A861 turned out to be not much more than a lane; in some places it became so narrow that passing bays were needed. There was so little traffic, however, that walking along the south bank of Loch Eil past the occasional dwelling and small wood was a pleasure.

At more than one point, when the road almost touched the lapping water, Jo took Stephen's hand and they stood gazing across the Loch at the attractive range of low mountains in the north. The water sparkled under the early afternoon sun and everything looked friendly and peaceful.

"How wide do you think the Loch is?" she asked.

"I know from the map that it runs west for just over six miles," Stephen replied. "It looks less than a mile wide here."

They marched on, only occasionally having to mount the verge to allow a car or tractor to pass. Eventually, the road curved north beyond the end of the Loch and went under a railway bridge before joining the A830. There was now quite a lot of traffic and it was with some relief that they arrived at the little guesthouse just outside Glenfinnan.

"That's one advantage of arriving at half past four!" Jo remarked, when she found that they had the shared bathroom to themselves.

Shortly before they left to walk into the village, Stephen outlined the plan for the following day. From Glenfinnan to Arisaig, nearly 19 miles away, there was no footpath and the only road was the A830. At Arisaig, however, they could switch to an alternative minor road that wound its way north and only joined the A830 again for the last couple of miles into Mallaig.

"The total distance from here to Mallaig is about 28 miles," he explained. "There happens to be a train coming through Glenfinnan at 9:05. My suggestion is that we take it as far as the next station - Lochailort. This will cut out over half the main road and give us time to look at more of the coast if we see somewhere particularly nice. We have a room booked Wednesday and Thursday nights in a small place about one mile south of Mallaig."
......

At six o'clock, they walked the mile or so into Glenfinnan to see the monument raised to commemorate the site where Bonny Prince Charlie raised his standard to gather an army to invade England in 1745. Eight months later, after an initially successful campaign, he was finally defeated at Culloden and escaped to France.

"I suppose it was a convenient open space at the top of Loch Shiel to set up camp," Jo observed, "but there's something rather sad about the place." She gazed down the Loch for a moment before adding: "There's a sombre beauty about the whole scene even on a sunny day!"

"It must be because the hopes of Scotland to throw off the English yoke were shattered in the end. A lot of people have been killed over the centuries and it has left an unhappy legacy," Stephen said sadly.

They rejoined the main road and turned west to cross the River Finnan. Almost immediately, he guided her down a narrow lane on the left.

"There's a hotel called Glenfinnan House just along here that must have lovely views over the Loch. We can get a cold drink and sit at an outside table. If the food is too expensive, we can move on and join the A830 again a short distance further west where there's another hotel."

"The fish at lunchtime was very sustaining," Jo assured him. "I'll be quite happy with a cold drink and sandwich, perhaps followed by coffee? We have a couple of bananas back at the guesthouse."

It was so pleasant sitting outside the hotel on a gravel terrace overlooking a wide expanse of grass with the water beyond that Stephen decided to order a bar meal before finishing off with coffee in the late evening sunshine.

"Thank you for another splendid day," Jo whispered, as they stood together beside the water afterwards.

Stephen bent to kiss her upturned face and she dreamily leaned her head against his shoulder for a few minutes in complete silence, just delighting in being together.

Chapter 14: Road to Mallaig

8:50 on Wednesday morning saw Stephen and Jo in Glenfinnan station yard looking at an old restaurant car.

"I bet that's a good tourist attraction," Jo said.

"I'm sure it is," Stephen answered. "I would've brought you here last night for a meal but it's not open in the evening."

"Never mind, you took me to a nice hotel with a lovely outlook."

The train journey west to Lochailort was quite short but the scenery delightful. Both the railway and the main road ran along a wooded valley flanked by rocky hills. For about half the journey, the train travelled close to the south bank of Loch Eilt with the A830 on the opposite bank.

At Jo's smart pace it did not take the young couple long to leave the small village well behind them. Although the gravel and grass verges on the A830 were narrow, they were well-maintained and protected by continuous white lines edging the road. In places, the rocky hillside had been cut away and pedestrians almost had to brush the rock face; in others, the ground dropped away from the road so sharply that there were stretches of protective metal barrier.

"This is a really good walk but would be quite brilliant if we were on something like the West Highland Way with no traffic!" Jo said at one point when there was a beautiful expanse of water to the left of the road.

"That's one of several sea lochs we'll be passing," Stephen commented.

After five miles or so they passed the isolated station of Beesdale at a point where the road ran alongside the railway.

"There doesn't even seem to be a hamlet, let alone a village, so where do the passengers live?" Jo asked.

"There must be a few houses and farmsteads tucked away somewhere," he surmised.

About a mile later, the young couple were delighted when a narrow pavement suddenly appeared on one side of the road.

"This is much better," Jo said as she speeded up appreciably.

The pavement continued for over two miles all the way to the outskirts of Arisaig, where Stephen guided her down a turning on the left.

"This is the B8008 and goes through the village before winding its way up the coast to Morar, back on the A830," he said. "It's high time we found some coffee!"

They walked on along the narrow road past a few houses and rounded a bend. Stretched out before them was a large expanse of water with a profusion of small boats moored in the distance.

"Another sea loch; quite tidal by the look of it," Stephen commented, just as they spotted the Arisaig Hotel on the right-hand side of the road.

......

Not long after one o'clock, the young couple left the hotel to walk the remaining nine miles to Mallaig.

"We've plenty of time to make a few detours whenever you see something interesting," Stephen said.

The road soon left the end of the sea loch and wound through attractive countryside for a couple of miles before slowly approaching the coast again and running alongside a narrow beach of pale sand strewn with seaweed. A strong sea breeze sent small clouds scudding across the sky.

"This is the sea proper now," Stephen commented.

"It's lovely!" Jo said, holding out her hand invitingly to encourage him to leave the road with her.

They walked along the beach and clambered over the rocky outcrops in search of small pools of trapped water containing fragments of seaweed and tiny sea creatures.

"This takes me back to my childhood and seaside holidays with my parents!" Stephen enthused.

"That's something I missed of course," Jo replied sadly. "I've only been to the seaside twice in my life when my foster parents took me on day trips to Brighton by train; the beach there is mainly pebbles unfortunately."

Stephen, sorry he had thoughtlessly mentioned seaside holidays, hugged her and whispered: "I'll give you a proper seaside holiday one day soon; I've heard that the island of Jersey is lovely."

Jo thanked him with a kiss as they reluctantly returned to the road. Another two miles followed with occasional glimpses of the water as they passed through a combination of open country, pleasant woods and beside rocky bracken-covered ridges. Then, after cresting a slight rise, the road turned inland beside a rock-strewn hill.

The steep slope was protected by a rather dilapidated wire fence and a profusion of low bushes. Jo soon spotted a pedestrian gate beside a larger one for cattle.

"Look; a kissing gate!" she exclaimed. "That presumably means walkers are allowed to go up the hill to see the view."

"I guess so," Stephen said as he helped her through the little swing gate.

They followed the faint track between clumps of bracken and outcrops of rock until there was a good view well out to sea. A sizeable island lay a few miles to the southwest.

"I think that must be the Isle of Eigg," Stephen said. "However, I'm fairly certain that the larger land mass to the northwest is Skye."

After a happy time just being together on such a lovely spot, they returned to the road and soon passed an almost white stretch of sand beside what looked like a river. A long bridge carried the railway across the placid water a short distance ahead.

Stephen looked at his map. "This river connects Loch Morar to the sea," he reported.

A few minutes later, the road crossed over the main A830 via a double T-junction and almost immediately crossed the river and went under the railway.

Stephen indicated a lane on the right-hand side. "We can do a slight detour here if you'd like to see Loch Morar?"

"Let's do that; I love lochs!" Jo replied.

They followed the river for a short distance until it entered the Loch. The lane then ran along the shoreline, giving the walkers a superb view.

"It's actually about 12 miles long," Stephen said, "although that little group of islands up there conceals the fact from this vantage point. To get back to the B8008, we just need to carry on and turn left in about 20 yards."

A few minutes later, they were back on their old road and passing Morar station. Just opposite was a large hotel. "What about a pot of tea?" he said invitingly.

......

Half an hour later, Jo and Stephen continued their journey.

"Not far now," he said. "I guess the B8008 is the original road to Mallaig because a short distance up here it joins the A830 for a mile before turning right and taking a parallel route into the town. Our guesthouse is not far past that turning."

"It's a good job it's not far," Jo remarked, looking up at the sky. The weather had been deteriorating gradually for well over an hour, but, during the short time they had been having tea, there were rain clouds as far as the eye could see.

The threat of rain forced them to increase speed after reaching the A830. A large section of the road cut through a rocky ridge, and, although rough underfoot, allowance had been made for pedestrians.

It began to drizzle for the last two hundred yards of the journey and two very relieved young couple rang the doorbell of the guesthouse soon after four-thirty.

......

An hour and a half later, Jo and Stephen left their small but comfortable room in the guesthouse and walked the remaining mile into Mallaig. It was raining steadily and they were clad in full waterproofs.

"At least we're not cluttered up with rucksacks!" Jo said, trying to look on the bright side.

The B8008 ran directly into the town centre opposite what looked like a pier for fishing boats. A signpost indicated that the station and ferry terminal were to the left. Tourists were hurrying around trying to avoid the rain, many looking for pubs and restaurants for their evening meal.

"What about the pub we passed a minute ago?" Jo suggested. "The sign mentioned fresh local fish dishes and it looks like the sort of place that wouldn't mind our wet gear."

It turned out to be a good suggestion; they had a nice meal in friendly surroundings. Afterwards, it was too wet to explore the town and so they returned to the guesthouse for an early night because the first ferry to Skye was due to leave at 8:40.

"It's a good job that most guesthouses in this part of the world have a room where you can leave things to dry out," Jo said, as they trudged through the wet gloom.

Chapter 15: Over the Sea to Skye

Jo stood at the rail of the car ferry with the eager anticipation of one who has never been to sea. The strong breeze caught strands of rich brown shoulder-length hair and swept it across her delighted face.

The deck heaved gently in the swell and the unaccustomed movement caused her to increase her grip on the handrail. A strong arm encircled her waist and she looked up at Stephen with a happy smile.

"Wind, rain or shine, she always looks adorable," he thought.

As it happened, the weather was looking extremely promising after all the rain the previous evening and night. Small clouds hid the sun from time to time, but, at the moment, the water was sparkling in the bright light.

"Perhaps the waves are dancing for joy!" This very odd thought had come to Jo out of the blue. Although she immediately dismissed it as nonsense, she was feeling just as bubbly inside as she had shortly before Stephen asked her to marry him. She found herself humming a faintly remembered tune and wondered if it had some connection with Skye.

"Isn't there a popular song about Skye?" she asked her companion.

"Yes, it's called "Over the sea to Skye"," Stephen replied. "It's a Gaelic rowing song believed to have originated when Bonnie Prince Charlie was being taken to Skye from one of the outer islands during his escape to France by some tortuous route. There are different versions of the words, but the chorus of the more popular one ends with: "Carry the lad that is born to be King over the sea to Skye". One of the verses mourns the men who were killed at Culloden."

The phrase "born to be King" struck a chord with Jo, but she had the odd feeling it had nothing to do with the Bonnie Prince.

......

The 30-minute voyage was over all too soon and they disembarked at Armadale and followed the coast road northeast.

"Skye is a surprisingly large island and really needs to be seen by car or by staying for several days," Stephen said. "We're on a peninsula about twelve miles long and five miles wide in the southwest corner. All we can do in seven hours is to see a small part of it. I suggest we follow this coast road for two miles and then take a left turn on to a minor road that cuts across the peninsula. According to Google Maps, the road reaches about 200m after two and a half miles and then a further half mile takes us down beside Loch Dhughaill."

It was not long before they passed the entrances of Skye Visitor Centre and Armadale Castle. "I made a note of a short walk that leaves from near here and is said to be quite scenic," Stephen commented.

"Perhaps on our way back to the ferry," Jo said.

The road ran beside the water for most of the next mile and a half. There was a dedicated walkway on the seaward side protected by white lines or a narrow pavement. Every so often, they stopped to gaze out across the water at the Scottish mainland about five miles away.

......

When they reached the minor road that Stephen had selected for their inland excursion, they were surprised to see a large group of buildings standing at the junction with the coast road; a signboard announced "Sabhal Mor Ostaig".

"I didn't expect to see anything like this here. I wonder what it is," Jo said.

Two people were coming out of the entrance and Stephen enquired about the buildings and was told that they contained film studios and teaching facilities for students learning the art of film making. The complex was part of a small higher education college a little further up the coast road.

"That makes perfect sense," Stephen said, as they walked up the narrow road. "Skye must be a fantastic place for wild and atmospheric backdrops. I've heard it was used for the films "Stardust" and "Snow White and the Huntsman"; both have been on TV several times."

The almost empty road up into the hills turned out to be the highlight of the morning's walk. Lower down, they passed the occasional farm and fields in which sheep grazed peacefully amongst the coarse grass and bracken, but, as the road climbed higher, the sheep became fewer and bracken was replaced by heather and rocks. The young couple really felt they were out in the wilds, especially when a cloud concealed the sun for several minutes and Jo took Stephen's hand, almost as if seeking his protection.

He looked down at her with delight but all she said was: "It's a good job you had the foresight to pack some water and a couple of bananas in your rucksack!"

......

Loch Dhughaill lay tranquil under the bright sun and they thoroughly enjoyed walking beside the water before climbing the slope that overlooked it and sitting in the warmth with their modest refreshments.

The downhill journey back to the coast road was covered surprisingly quickly. On arrival, Stephen turned north.

"I know there's a good café back in the Visitor Centre which would probably be a good place for a lunchtime snack if it's not too crowded," he said, "but it would be nice to find coffee somewhere nearer first. There's a small village just over half a mile up the road – at least Google shows a church there."

"It's a pleasant walk anyway," Jo said cheerfully.

It was not long before they passed the entrance of Sabhal Mor Ostaig College; it appeared to be a newly built white building in a lovely position overlooking the sea.

"What a lovely place to be a student!" Jo exclaimed. She felt the same when they almost immediately passed a primary school.

The modest grey-stone Church of Scotland building stood on the seaward side of the road. Opposite was a narrow road that ran inland, flanked by a bus shelter and letter box. Only one house was visible from the main road.

"Let's go a short distance up the lane anyway; we may be in luck!" Stephen said.

However, it only took about a hundred yards to reveal that the tiny village only consisted of the church and a few scattered dwellings.

"People must come from the houses widely scattered along the coast," Jo surmised.

"And possibly the College if some students live on site," Stephen added.

They turned and walked back down the slope. They were just about to pass the entrance to the track leading up to the house near the main road when an old man came out laboriously pushing a large wheelbarrow piled high with chopped logs. As he turned to go downhill, the barrow tipped sideways and logs were scattered everywhere.

The young couple hurried to help. Stephen righted the large barrow and helped Jo and the old man refill it, while the latter gave them what sounded like profuse thanks for their help. Unfortunately, it was almost impossible to understand him.

"That's really kind of you!" a voice called from behind them.

They all looked back to see a young man, not much older than Stephen, coming down the slope. He was wearing a dog-collar. "He must be the vicar or minister," Jo thought.

"Angus always tries to carry too much in that rickety old barrow of his; I think it has a square wheel!" the young man continued with a friendly smile. He patted the old man on the back affectionately. "He's the salt of the earth; our little church would be lost without him! Those logs are for our church furnace."

The old man gave him an almost toothless grin and muttered something. He could obviously understand what was being said even if his own speech needed an interpreter.

"Are you staying on the Island?" the young man asked.

"No, just on a day trip from Mallaig," Stephen replied, shaking the offered hand.

"In fact, we've walked most of the way from just outside Stirling," Jo volunteered. "We joined the West Highland Way near Crianlarich."

"I'm impressed!" the young man said. "I can tell you're from the south of England. You speak almost exactly like my wife. We've only been married two and a half years and she grew up in Newbury."

"We're from the Reading area," Stephen said. "I'll push the wheelbarrow to your wood store. If you could all take a couple of logs each it would make the load easier."

The small procession crossed the coast road and the young minister opened the wrought-iron gate to lead them around the back of the building. Leaving the old man to the skilled task of stacking the cut logs neatly, he unlocked the side entrance of the building. "Do let me show you round," he said.

As they followed him inside, he continued: "My wife would love to meet two young people from her part of the world. I obtained a degree in electrical engineering at Glasgow University before studying for the ministry at Trinity College. I married Sally halfway through my final year. The poor girl never dreamt that my first placement would be at a small church in Skye; it's been difficult for her to adjust to the remoteness of this place, although it helps to be near the mainland. One of the reasons I was sent here is that part of my stipend is covered by the part-time teaching I do at the College just down the road; they were desperate for somebody with my engineering background."

He paused and looked at them hopefully. "If you can spare the time, would you like to join us for something to eat? We're only having a sort of ploughman's lunch: freshly baked bread and cheese with pickle and salad trimmings?"

"Thank you; we'd love to come," Jo said immediately.

"We have a ferry to catch at 16:45 and would also like to visit that splendid-looking Visitor Centre," Stephen added, more cautiously.

"That's no problem; it's only 12:35 now and I can give you a lift for the two miles down to the Centre. I'm Michael, by the way."

"Jo and Stephen," the latter replied, gesturing to his smiling companion.

Jo was feeling strangely excited. She began to look around the small building while Michael went into the vestry to telephone his wife and warn her about the unexpected guests.

"She only needs to slice an extra couple of tomatoes," he said as he closed the door.

Jo wandered down the aisle. There was a nicely embroidered banner to one side of the Communion Table and she went over to look at it. Beautifully stitched on the centre panel were the words: "Behold, now is the accepted time; behold, now is the day of salvation. (2 Cor. 6:2)".

She was unable to take her eyes off it. "Stephen, come and look at this!" she called.

He came to stand beside her. "This is extraordinary!" he muttered. "I didn't even believe in the existence of God three days ago, but now we've heard audible words on a remote path, seen exactly the same words in a Bible that just happened to be open at the correct page and now been confronted with this exhortation. It can't all be a coincidence; Sarah's explanation begins to make sense to me!"

"Mrs Driscol was most apologetic that lack of space meant she had to use the abbreviation "Cor" instead of "Corinthians"," Michael said from behind them.

The young couple looked at him blankly and he hurried to explain further. "2 Corinthians refers to St Paul's second letter to the Christian community in the Greek city of Corinth."

Then he saw that they still looked bewildered. "There's something much more critical worrying you, isn't there? Come and tell us over lunch. Sally is just as discrete as I have to be in my profession."

"Yes, I believe we need to tell you what happened on a lonely stretch of the West Highland Way near Black Mount," Jo said, as they all turned to go.

The minister's house, or manse, was only a hundred yards up the narrow road opposite the church. Sally welcomed them warmly on arrival. A few minutes later, she took them into a pleasant kitchen where a simple meal had been laid out on the table. A small toddler, strapped in his high chair, was waving a spoon vigorously, having just finished eating something from a plastic dish.

Towards the end of the simple repast, Sally excused herself to put little Josh in his cot for an afternoon nap.

"That's better," she said when she returned. "It's been lovely sharing reminisces with you about our shared home territory but now I'll just pour us all another cup of tea and then you can tell us what's troubling you. If you don't mind me being here, that is? Michael has a study you could go in."

"We're very happy to share with you both," Jo replied quickly.

As it turned out, she and Stephen found it surprisingly easy to share their recent experiences with such a friendly couple in a relaxed environment. When Stephen finished his contribution by admitting that his earlier resistance started melting while looking at the banner in the church, Michael nodded.

"I'm absolutely certain that God is seeking to draw you into a loving relationship," he said slowly. "Verse 6 you saw in Chapter 14 of St John's Gospel makes it crystal clear that no one can come to God the Father except through the death of Jesus on the Cross, however hard it is for people to accept such an exclusive claim."

"After all," Sally added, "if there was an easier way, don't you think God would have spared Jesus such an appalling experience? The love of Jesus for men and women is so great that he was prepared to pay the price."

She put her hand over Jo's as it lay on the table. "God has invited you and now he's effectively saying that the time is ripe for you to make a decision. Are you two prepared to accept his offer?"

Jo looked at Stephen; she was reluctant to take any step without him. He answered for her. "Yes, we are," he declared firmly, "but we don't know how to do it."

Sally and Michael beamed with pleasure. "That's easy," he said. "Just confess that you've been busy going your own way and completely ignored your Maker, say you're sorry and ask for his forgiveness, declare that you believe Jesus died on the Cross for you and ask him to be your Saviour and help you lead a life pleasing to him. I'll lead you in a short prayer if you like. Just repeat each sentence aloud after me. God looks at the heart; the exact words don't matter."

"Do we need to kneel down?" Jo asked.

Michael shook his head. "Only kneel down if it would help you. Otherwise just sit comfortably with your head bowed and eyes closed to avoid distraction."

The prayer he proceeded to pray, pausing for them to repeat his words, seemed just right. Jo, in particular, found it helpful that Sally joined in the repetition; there was something rather beautiful about the way she identified with two almost complete strangers.

At the conclusion of the prayer there was an almost palpable atmosphere of peace in the room and both Jo and Stephen had a feeling of lightness inside. Then Sally did another beautiful thing; having learned earlier that they were both orphans, she prayed very movingly that God would heal them of all the hurt this had entailed and enable them to experience him as their Father.

......

A little later, Jo and Stephen got ready to leave the happy home. They exchanged email addresses with their new friends and Sally produced two small booklets from a drawer in the kitchen dresser.

"Here's a copy of St Mark's Gospel and a short Bible reading guide for new Christians," she said. "Although beautiful, the language of the old King James' version is sometimes difficult to understand; it's probably better to find a more modern translation. Most good bookshops will have a selection and this little booklet makes two or three suggestions."

There were hugs all round and Sally walked down to the coast road with them, leaving Michael to get on with his Sunday sermon. "When you next come to Skye – hopefully for more than a day trip – do let us know and we'll invite you to a proper meal," were her last parting words.

Jo and Stephen left her waving goodbye on the corner as they began their walk south to the Visitor Centre. "What a splendid couple!" Jo said. "We must choose a nice toy for the little lad as a thank-you for their kindness."

They walked along the seaward side of the road. Everything seemed brighter and more vibrant than when going in the opposite direction, although the weather was exactly the same mix of cloud and sunshine. For the first time since Jo had agreed to marry him, Stephen felt what Jo liked to describe as all bubbly inside.

Shortly after passing the film studio and narrow road that crossed the peninsula, he looked at his watch; it was two-fifty. "We've got just under two hours before the ferry," he said. "There's a path on the right fairly soon that winds its way up through the woods to the top of Armadale hill; the view is said to good. If we speed up, we should have time to drop down from there to the café in the Visitor Centre for a coffee before going back to the pier. What do you think?"

"You know me; I'm always game for a challenge. In fact, I'm feel so full of energy at the moment I could run all the way"

He laughed. "A good fast pace will be enough!"
......

The view from the top of the hill was certainly worth the effort. There was something special about being able to look down over the coast and sea at quite close quarters.

After a couple of minutes, Jo was able to satisfy her desire to run as they both scampered down the mile-long path to the

Visitor Centre, somewhat to the amusement of visitors climbing up in the opposite direction.

After a cup of coffee in the surprisingly attractive café, they hurried to catch the ferry.

Towards the end of the short voyage, Stephen's 'phone rang; it was the detective constable from Stirling giving him a brief update.

"Thanks to the excellent facial composite Fort William sent through, we managed to track down and arrest that thug late this morning for attempted kidnap," the faint voice reported. "During our questioning, I emphasized how very shaken the young lady was by the attack but said I would do all I could to persuade her not to press charges in exchange for all the information he could give me about the so-called Professor Makin.

"As a result, he's been very cooperative. He informed me that the fake professor is not part of a gang but works on his own, only hiring the occasional help, and that he's been employed twice, the first time as a straightforward bodyguard. The rumour in the Stirling underworld is that the man only deals in small high-value items, has a reputation for being ruthless and is as slippery as an eel! So far, we've no idea where he is or what he's up to. He had almost recovered from his fall by the time our thug had driven him back to Stirling and dropped him in the city centre before dumping the car in a suburb.

"Don't alarm your girl but take great care, especially while you're still in Scotland; I've a nasty feeling this unpleasant specimen has not given up trying to get this valuable file and believes you may have kept a copy. Have you?"

"No, I deleted it from my notebook soon after you told me the contents of the memory stick had been safely transferred to the Thames Valley police," Stephen assured him.

"That's good. I can't see how our man could possibly trace you, but get in touch with us immediately if you see any sign of him; his picture and finger prints have been circulated throughout Scotland. Keep safe!"

For obvious reasons, Stephen only gave Jo the first part of this report and was glad that they then had the distraction of looking around an unfamiliar area. It was only twenty past five and so they first took the road that went east beside the harbour and then curved north along the coast. Pleasant bungalows and houses overlooked the sea for well over half a mile before reaching open country and it was clear that the road formed the most desirable residential part of the town. In the end, the young couple walked for about a mile before turning back to explore some of the back streets of what turned out to be a surprisingly small town centre.

At about six-thirty, they ended up in a small restaurant called the Cornerstone and had an excellent fish stew with some of the best vegetables they had come across so far.

After returning to the guesthouse for their last night, Jo suggested that they try praying together. Feeling very awkward and uncertain at first, and not really knowing how to address God, they eventually tried imagining that Jesus was in the room with them. In a few short sentences, they simply expressed what was on their hearts; grateful thanks for his audible words on the lonely path and then the step-by-step sequence of events that had led up to the encounter with Sarah in Kinlochleven and Michael and Sally on Skye.

"Lord Jesus, I don't really understand why you chose to call us or how you arranged to bring all this about," Jo whispered at one point, "but thank you that you included us amongst those you suffered so much for on the Cross."

When they fell silent after a few minutes, they became aware that the atmosphere in the bedroom had changed; there seemed to be a loving presence surrounding them and Jo even began to sob gently as some of the hurts of the past rose to the surface of her memory and then melted away.

Stephen got quite concern until she eventually turned to him with a shining face and said: "I think I'm being healed of some of my hurtful memories!"

He took her in his arms and they shared the joy of this revelation together.

A little later, after a cup of hot chocolate downstairs with several other guests, they went to bed and slept peacefully until Stephen's little alarm clock sounded at 7:30.

Chapter 16: Homeward bound

The first train of the day to Fort William left Mallaig at 10:10. The 80-minute journey through a beautiful sunlit landscape was sheer pleasure and the young couple were almost sorry when the train trundled through the extensive western suburbs of the town.

Leaving the busy station, they followed a pedestrian walkway down to the northern end of the High Street, purchasing two packets of sandwiches and a few other things at a Tesco Express en route. Once in the short street, where they had visited the police station only three days before, they started to look for somewhere for a drink.

"It's nearly midday; a hotel might be better and less crowded than a café," Jo suggested. A minute later, she spotted the West End Hotel. "Let's go in there."

After a comfortable coffee stop, they retraced their steps past the station in the direction of Glen Nevis. Stephen's aim was to walk beside the River Nevis for just over two miles, find somewhere for another short refreshment stop, and then join the West Highland Way to climb up to the junction where it rejoined the Old Military Road. After that, they would be on a familiar path back to Kinlochleven.

The road up Glen Nevis was obviously a popular walking route for people staying in the area and even had a pavement on one side for the first two miles. It would have been a really splendid walk up the river valley if it had not been for the trees that frequently obscured the view.

"The mountain to the left of us on the other side of the river is a mere 700m, but we should soon be able to get a view of Ben Nevis, the highest mountain in the UK at 1345m," Stephen informed his eager companion. "It's roughly to the southeast of us."

A little later, Jo slapped her arm. "I'm glad someone at the hotel warned us to apply plenty of insect repellent! Mine is having a struggle to cope with all these midges."

"I suppose people who live and work here just have to put up with multiple bites until their blood becomes less tasty to the little blighters!" he replied.

It was not long before they came to a larger area of open ground with a small car park and a single-storey building with a sign board announcing "Glen Nevis Restaurant and Bar". A narrow road ran down beside the building.

"We can join the West Highland Way by going down this little road. However, let's walk on another quarter mile or so in the hope of getting a better view of Ben Nevis before coming back here for a cold drink," Stephen suggested.

"We mustn't take more than half an hour in total," Jo reminded him. "Sarah is expecting us in Kinlochleven at six-thirty and we're taking her for a thank-you meal at the Tailrace Inn tonight."

The short extra distance was worth the effort. Ben Nevis almost seemed to tower above them, although it was further from the road than the lower mountain they had passed earlier.

"It looks particularly high because we're almost at sea level," Stephen said.
......

By two o'clock, the young couple were walking down the narrow road past a few scattered houses to join a path going up through the woods on the western slopes of Glen Nevis to join the West Highland Way on its way south towards Kinlochleven.

Once on the latter, they climbed gradually through a mixture of woodland and more open ground to a height of about 280m before dropping down slightly. The path then wound its way through an attractive valley between two ridges. At one point, where there was a splendid view of Ben Nevis framed by a smaller mountain on one side and trees on the other, they stopped to have the sandwiches bought in Fort William.

"It was worth seeing Glen Nevis and the highest mountain in the UK, but it's not as beautiful as some of the other places we've seen this week," Jo said.

96

They were almost surprised by how quickly they reached the point at which the Way rejoined the Old Military Road. From here they were marching over familiar ground. By only pausing briefly for the occasional drink of water, they were on the outskirts of Kinlochleven and passing the little church, now etched firmly in their memories, soon after half past six.

"We've not done too badly!" Jo exclaimed with some satisfaction.

......

Sarah greeted them with a delight that almost overflowed when they told her briefly what had happened in Skye.

"Come, let me hug you both," she cried with tears of joy in her eyes. "I've been praying for you every day."

Jo was so moved that she remained hugging the old woman while she whispered: "Your prayers were answered. Thank you from the bottom of my heart!"

It was a happy little group that walked slowly to the Tailrace Inn. Jo could sense that Sarah was already enjoying the novelty of being taken out for a meal, even at a place so close to home.

"Fred came here for a drink most Friday evenings after he'd been paid," she said nostalgically. "On special occasions he would bring me and we'd have a drink and a steak and kidney pie or something but never a two-course meal. You're really spoiling me!"

"Jo and I owe you a debt we can never repay," Stephen replied, suddenly feeling a surge of affection for their new friend.

......

After everyone had enjoyed a good meal and they were finishing with a hot drink, Stephen took out his little notebook to use the pub's Wi-Fi system to consult the railway timetable.

Sarah, who had never seen a computer at close quarters before, watched with fascination while he typed "Bridge of Orchy" and "Crianlarich" into the two boxes on the screen, together with the day and approximate time of departure, and then waited a few seconds for the result.

"There's only one possibility, unfortunately," he reported. "There's a train coming through from Fort William at 18:58. I'll have to 'phone the guesthouse I've booked on the northern edge of Crianlarich to say that we won't be able to get there until after half past seven."

"We could walk on to Tyndrum and have some refreshments at the Real Food Café before joining the same train soon after seven; or we could walk all the way!"

Stephen grinned at Jo's enthusiasm. "I know you're a terrific walker but I think a total of about 32 miles to Crianlarich is a bit too much!"

Sarah nodded in agreement. "You mustn't overdo things, my dear," she said. "I'll make sure I get breakfast really early so that you can enjoy the hike and not have to rush. I've got some bacon this time!"

They walked back to Sarah's house and she insisted on making a pot of tea. While they sat in her little parlour, they told her a little more about what had happened on Skye.

Sarah was delighted that Michael and Sally had been so hospitable and helpful. "Just think," she said. "If that old man hadn't spilt his logs you wouldn't have gone to help him or met Michael. I never cease to wonder at the way God brings these things about!"

She paused before going on. "If I may give you some advice; trust Jesus to guide you, find a friendly church that believes the Bible is the Word of God and get into the habit of praying regularly, both separately and together."

"Sally gave us a copy of St Mark's Gospel and we're going to get a Bible as soon as possible," Jo said.

Then it occurred to her to mention that the song "Over the sea to Skye" had come to her while they were on the ferry and Stephen had managed to quote part of the chorus: "Carry the lad that is born to be King over the sea to Skye".

"For some reason the phrase "born to be King" kept coming back to me all that day," she told Sarah. "But somehow I knew it had nothing to do with Bonnie Prince Charlie!"

Sarah looked at her. "You know who really was born to be King, don't you?"

The young couple looked at her and shook their heads.

"It was Jesus; two thousand years ago he came as Saviour but the Bible makes very clear that the next time he will come as King."

Then a happy memory came back to her. "Years ago," she reminisced, "Fred and I joined a coach trip organized by the local churches to go to Fort William to see the choral society there perform Handel's Messiah. I'll never forget that wonderful experience, especially the Hallelujah Chorus when the whole audience stands to its feet. The words are truly inspired and inspiring!"

She closed her eyes as if experiencing it again and began to sing, quietly at first but becoming stronger: "King of kings and Lord of lords – King of kings and Lord of lords – And He shall reign forever and ever – Forever and ever – Hallelujah, Hallelujah, Hallelujah…. Wonderful, I thought my heart would burst for joy!"

There were tears in her eyes as she looked at them again. "Some of these phrases are taken from Chapter 19 of Revelation – the last book in the Bible – using the text of the old King James' version of course!"

"May we regard you as our honorary aunt?" Jo said suddenly. Then, as she saw tears well up in Sarah's eyes again, she gave her time to recover by adding: "I'll give you my mobile 'phone number now and let you know our address when we find a little flat in Swindon. Stephen starts his first job at the beginning of September and we plan to get married a few days before then."

"You've made an old woman even happier!" Sarah whispered and Jo stood up to hug her new aunt.

……

The young couple set out from Kinlochleven at 7:50 after an emotional farewell from Sarah, Jo having promised to write to her as soon as they had fixed the date of their wedding.

"Actually, I'm going to send Sarah a picture postcard as soon as I get back to Pangbourne," Jo said, as they joined the West Highland Way on their southbound journey.

The weather was much more settled than it had been when they were coming in the opposite direction: it was what is sometimes described as cloudy-bright. By half past ten, they were having a coffee stop at the King's House Hotel in readiness for the ten-mile hike past Glencoe Mountain Resort to a late lunch stop at the Inveroran Hotel.

With renewed energy, Jo set a fast pace as they set out again, only pausing briefly at the spot where Jesus had spoken to them on the northbound journey. They felt drawn to give thanks and marvel once again that he had used the exact words from the King James' Bible because he knew they would be driven into Sarah's little church by the downpour and see the full text in the open Bible on the lectern.

......

The two travellers arrived at the Inveroran Hotel shortly before two o'clock and were surprised to find quite a large number of walkers still having lunchtime refreshments in the bar. Three quarters of an hour later, feeling re-energised, they set out again.

"To save time, I suggest we stay on the Old Military Road rather than take the longer Highland Way path to Orchy," Stephen said.

Marching along the narrow road, not much more than a rough track in places, they soon turned to south to follow the river down to the stone bridge where they had stood after the celebration dinner on the day of their engagement. Stephen could not resist giving his fiancée a hug as they stood by the parapet once again.

As they went through the underpass at Bridge of Orchy station, he said: "It's barely half past three. We should be able to reach the Real Food Café in Tyndrum for tea and something to eat in less than two hours."

"The train doesn't reach Tyndrum until after seven o'clock. I'd be quite happy not to hang about after tea but walk all the way to Crianlarich," Jo replied cheerfully. "It's only another five miles and the guesthouse is on the northern outskirts anyway."

"We'll see how you feel after tea!"

......

As they went along the path below the slope on which Stephen had proposed to her only six days earlier, a surge of joy flooded Jo's heart. She took his hand and whispered: "Thank you for loving me."

She looked so adorable that Stephen just had to stop and draw her into a tight embrace. "You're the only girl in the world for me!" he said softly as he kissed her.

They were both so happy that they walked on as if in a dream; even the rather cloudy weather seemed to have brightened and the beautiful surroundings were even more so.

Consequently, it was almost with surprise that they found themselves emerging on to the main road in Tyndrum with the Real Food Café only a short distance away on the opposite side of the road.

Jo found it so hard to choose between a cream scone and a slice of cake that they had one of each and shared them. It was pleasant sitting in the friendly café, still popular even at five-thirty, enjoying a refreshing tea break.

In fact, she felt so refreshed that she insisted on walking the remaining distance to the guesthouse and not wasting time waiting for the train.

"However, I think it would be wise to take the direct route of four and a half miles along the road," Stephen said as they set out.

They were pleased to find that walkers were provided with a narrow gravel path for most of the way. As Jo had noticed on the

train when coming in the opposite direction, the scenery was a delightful mix of rolling countryside, small woods and distant hills.
......

They were walking up the drive of the guesthouse at a quarter to seven. It was situated in a peaceful garden and set back about 30 yards from the road; even better, their twin room had a small en-suite bathroom.

About fifty minutes later, feeling extremely hungry, they set out on the short walk into Crianlarich. The main road ran under a railway bridge and almost immediately passed Crianlarich Hotel.

"We need a decent meal; let's go in here," Stephen said. "This is my treat and I don't want you worrying about the cost!"

A friendly waitress showed them to a table. "You're just in time to take advantage of the fixed-price menu if you'd like it," she said. Jo grinned happily as she took the menu card.

"Oh good, there's carrot and coriander soup and one of the main courses is salmon!" she exclaimed quietly as soon as the waitress was out of earshot. "Please may I have both those? They've also got treacle sponge and custard for desert; something I haven't had for ages."

Stephen smiled indulgently; it was good to see her so full of life even after such a long trek. "You may have whatever you like."

It was a pleasant restaurant and a nice change from going to a crowded pub for a bar meal. The service was quite slow but they were in no hurry. After the meal, they relaxed even further by moving to the lounge area between the restaurant and the side entrance of the hotel for coffee.

They had been enjoying the evening so much that Jo was surprised when she realized it was ten o'clock.

"I suppose we'd better go back; we've got a long hike tomorrow," she said reluctantly as she slipped her arms into her anorak.

"It's about 26 miles: not as far as today but some of it is on very rough ground," Stephen explained. "There's a path from the village that links up with the West Highland Way. We can follow the latter south down the east bank of Loch Lomond. I think you watched me yesterday booking a room on my notebook at a lovely looking B and B called "The Shepherd's Rest" about three miles north of Balmaha. On Monday night, we'll stop somewhere in Milngavie at the end of the Way and then catch a train for the short journey into Glasgow early Tuesday morning. This will allow us some time to look around the city centre before catching the London train."

Chapter 17: An Unpleasant Surprise

Leaving through the side entrance of the hotel, they turned left to reach the main road and left again past the front of the building where the bar was situated. Glancing sideways, Jo saw a man at a window table drinking a glass of whisky and looking out into the gathering gloom.

To her horror, it was Professor Makin. The glass in his hand jerked as he recognized her.

She gasped and gripped Stephen's elbow to hurry him on. "Professor Makin is sitting at a window table in the bar and he's spotted me!" she said in a shocked whisper.

Stephen looked at her incredulously. "You're imagining things. It must be someone who looks similar; after all it's beginning to get dark."

"I'm absolutely positive," she insisted. "His glass jerked so violently that he probably spilt his drink!"

"Here of all places," Stephen muttered as he stopped under the railway bridge and took out his mobile and a small torch. "We must get an urgent message to Stirling. Please hold my torch so that I can read the 'phone number on that detective constable's business card. He's probably not in the office but somebody will be able to take action and send a police car."

The signal was poor but he managed to get his report across to somebody on duty. "A police car will be directed to the hotel immediately," he reported. "He wanted us to go and wait for it, but I've said I'll come back immediately I've got you safely to our guesthouse."

"I'll stay," Jo said, but was secretly rather pleased when Stephen insisted on hurrying her back towards the guesthouse; the thought of meeting Professor Makin face to face made her shiver.

They started running, and, in less than three minutes, Stephen was unlocking the front door. "Here's our room key. Please tell the couple who run the place what's happened if they're still around. Keep safe!" He gave her a kiss and disappeared.

By running all the way, he managed to get back to the hotel less than fifteen minutes after leaving it. The police car drew up almost before he had had time to get his breath back. He was thankful to find that the two officers had already downloaded a copy of the fake professor's facial composite on some sort of smartphone.

The three of them entered the hotel and made for the reception desk. The small facsimile was recognized immediately as a professional-looking man who had been in several times over the last two or three days, but he was not staying in the hotel and the barman confirmed that he had left very hurriedly a short time earlier.

While one policeman was obtaining a list of bed and breakfast places in the area from the assistant manager, Stephen apologized to the other one for not coming back into the building immediately after Jo had recognized the fake professor.

"It's best you didn't," the man replied. "We think he may be dangerous when confronted; Stirling are beginning to find clues linking him to other crimes. Please keep your eyes open and report any sighting immediately. In the meantime, I'll take a note of the address of your guesthouse and their 'phone number; the Stirling detective in charge of this case may want to contact you and mobile signals in this area are very variable."

"We'll be leaving at 8:00 to go south down the West Highland Way and so I'd also better give you the details of tomorrow night's guesthouse near Balmaha," Stephen said.

......

When he returned to the guesthouse he found Jo having a cup of hot chocolate in the kitchen with their kind hosts. She jumped up and threw her arms around him.

"You're safe; I've been so worried," she whispered as he hugged her tight.

He reported what had happened while he also had a hot drink and then they went up to bed. Before they could think of going to sleep, however, they just had to discuss the event a little further.

"I suppose it was quite a crafty move for him to lie low here in Crianlarich, not far from where he tried to accost you, and let the police waste their time searching in the Stirling area," Stephen surmised.

"The alternative scenario is that he may still be after a copy of the computer program he thinks we have!" Jo's voice trembled.

Stephen shook his head. "How could he be sure we were planning to come back this way? He would also need quite a lot of help to keep a proper watch and there's only one other crook who knows what we look like; he won't dare to get involved again!"

He was silent for a minute, deep in thought. Then he looked rather sheepish.

"I believe I know how he may have found out about our plans. It's entirely my fault! You remember he knew about the guesthouse in Stirling? Indeed, he may be the one who arranged it. Well, after breakfast on that first Friday morning, you went back to the bedroom to finish packing while I paid the additional charge for double occupancy. The landlady was very chatty and asked where we intended to go in Scotland. Foolishly I told her we were planning to join the West Highland Way near Crianlarich and go up to Mallaig and back before continuing to follow the Way south through the Trossacks to Glasgow."

"Well; just suppose, after recovering from his accident and now knowing that I was with you, our dear professor went to the guesthouse to enquire about us. He's a persuasive enough character to get her to part with the information about our plans. He has therefore positioned himself in Crianlarich both to hide from the police and in the hope of intercepting us on our way south."

"If you're right," Jo said, "then for the last couple of days he's been roaming up and down this section of the Way looking in every possible place we might be! What a horrible thought!"

106

Stephen took her in his arms. "I'm going to look after you," he whispered. "If that fellow so much as tries to lay a finger on you, I'll pulverize him!"

Jo smiled at this exaggeration but felt comforted by the fact that her fiancé was so protective of her. She showed her appreciation with a kiss.

"We need to pray for God's protection before we go to bed," she said.

......

Given the shock and excitement of the previous evening, they slept surprisingly well, although Jo awoke vaguely conscious that Professor Makin had appeared in her dreams more than once.

The weather was still gloomy when they set out at about eight o'clock but there were signs that the sun might break through later in the morning.

Stephen led Jo across the A82 and west up a fairly steep path to join a wide track that she surmised was probably the Old Military Road again.

"We've had to climb all the way up here before dropping down again towards the valley of the River Fallock. I believe its source is somewhere south of Crianlarich and it takes a sharp turn near here to run down into Loch Lomond," he told her as they marched along at a rapid pace.

Jo was happy to go at almost any speed; the possibility that Professor Makin might be on patrol in the vicinity was an unpleasant thought and she found herself glancing back the way they had come.

It was difficult for her to imagine him covering long distances on foot – motorized transport was more his style – but she had the uncomfortable feeling that his anger at being thwarted was sufficiently strong for him to spend time and money taking some sort of revenge, even if he now had relatively little hope of getting a copy of the stolen software.

She was startled when she felt a hand on her elbow, but it was only Stephen guiding her left off the track and down a rough narrow path that descended towards the valley floor.

"The Way drops down here to go under the main road and then across the railway to reach the north bank of the river and follow it for some distance," he said. "I suppose the Old Military Road we've been using must peter out for a bit before starting again later."

"Or it may now be a private road," Jo guessed.

They were certainly descending quickly because she found herself going down a very long flight of steps set into the slope and aiming for a tunnel under the road. Although care was necessary to avoid slipping, she fleetingly noticed a motorbike propped against the safety barrier with its rider, wearing crash helmet and goggles, standing consulting a map.

A few moments of relative darkness and they were out in the open again gazing towards a particularly attractive range of mountains. They climbed over a stile, went under the railway, and then followed the river as it tossed and bubbled its way through the trees. Less than a mile later, the path took them over a footbridge to the south side of the river and joined a farm track coming from the main road.

Passing the small white farmhouse, they hurried on for another mile or so over a succession of stiles, gates and small streams, the latter feeding the river, now slightly further away to their right.

"We're about to pass fairly close to the Falls of Fallock: a waterfall and some rapids in a shallow gorge," Stephen reported. "I believe there's a car park and observation point that can be accessed from the A82. Unfortunately, we haven't really got time to investigate even if we could get off this path."

"Yes, I believe we'll have to slow down along the bank of Loch Lomond," Jo said. "Somebody at breakfast this morning said that it's a surprisingly rough and narrow path – quite a scramble!"

......

Less than a mile later, a wide gap in the trees gave them a clear view of the A82, now much closer than before, and a track that departed from the road to cut across their path and continue southward. To their surprise, there was no sign of the river.

"The Fallock must have turned north under the road somewhere this side of the Falls," Stephen said.

As soon as they crossed the track to continue along the Highland Way, Jo's sharp eyes spotted flashes of light reflected from fast running water; the river had just emerged from under the road accompanied by its usual screen of bushes and small trees.

"Here it is again!" she exclaimed, almost as if she was pleased to see a familiar friend. She was soon to be very grateful for its presence.

As she spoke, the peace was broken by the full-throated roar of a motorbike starting up somewhere on the road; it could then be heard turning off the road and entering the track they had just crossed. The young couple did not pay much attention until there was a loud cry behind them and they spun round to see a young man, who had just passed them going in the opposite direction, leaping to one side as the motorbike stormed past him. It was now only a few yards away and aiming straight for them.

Stephen pushed Jo to one side and tried to use his body to shield her.

"Jesus!" she cried in desperation.

What happened next was quite extraordinary.

Chapter 18: Deliverance

The motorbike's wheels locked completely solid. The astonished onlookers saw the rider shoot over the handlebars, plunge headfirst through the foliage and slither down the narrow bank into the river. Meanwhile the bike, still upright, skidded past and buried itself in a bush.

For a second, the young couple were frozen with shock. Then it dawned on Jo that they had been saved by a miracle.

"Thank you, Jesus!" she whispered. "Now please help us rescue the rider."

The young man rushed up to them. "That motorcyclist looked as if he intended to run you down but then decided to brake at the last moment!" he exclaimed in amazement.

But there was no time to waste. All three of them scrambled down to the water's edge. The rider was spread-eagled face down in the shallow water with one leg and arm still in contact with the muddy bank.

The two men dragged the prostrate figure to safety and turned him over, coughing and spluttering. With difficulty, they managed to remove his helmet and full-face visor. The man was now making a horrible gurgling noise as he desperately tried to suck in air.

"Quick, he's choking! Turn him over and try to get him on his hands and knees so he can cough up the water," Jo said urgently. "It's Professor Makin," she added, registering no surprise.

By now the two men had helped the fake professor to get on all fours and he was coughing up river water in frantic spasms of retching.

As Jo watched, ready to thump the stricken man's back if necessary, she noticed Stephen quietly explaining to their helper that the motorcyclist was wanted by the police and it would be a great help if he could stay on guard until they arrived. The young man looked surprised but nodded and Stephen turned away to use his mobile 'phone.

The fits of coughing became less frequent and Jo relaxed slightly. She even began to feel rather sorry for the thoroughly shocked, shaken and bedraggled man. His heavy leather jacket and trousers were badly scuffed, his gauntlets were a virtual write-off and the area around him was scattered with bits torn from the bushes edging the river bank. Nevertheless, the dense foliage and his protective clothing had saved him from serious injury.

It was not long before she was delegated to stand on the side of the road to meet the patrol car and act as a guide.

When she had gone, the fake professor spoke for the first time. "You two wretched pests have ruined my chances of selling that software for a lot of money," he growled hoarsely and then had another fit of coughing.

"Our only copy was given to the police in Stirling and so it's no good keeping on chasing us," Stephen said firmly. "You nearly ran all three of us down, but I suggest we don't press charges in exchange for you agreeing to cooperate with the police about the attempted theft."

"I'll consider it," their captive said truculently. "Help me get back on the path; I think I can just about walk."

"Don't attempt to escape," the helpful young man said angrily. "I've got the key of your motorbike. You're very lucky these generous folk are not going to get you charged with attempting to cause them grievous bodily harm! I can bear witness to your obvious intent if it becomes necessary."

......

Jo appeared, followed by two policemen. One smiled broadly when he verified who the detained person was and produced a pair of handcuffs. The other took out a notebook and gave the bedraggled figure the customary caution.

Jo, seeing that Professor Makin was now able to stand unaided, gave a sigh of relief and quickly reported what she had already told the two policemen, hoping it did not conflict with anything Stephen might have said on the 'phone.

"I've explained that the motorbike was going dangerously fast on this narrow path, and, when it braked hard, the rider came off over the handlebars. We were then surprised to find that it was the fake professor and realized he still believed we had kept a copy of the stolen computer coding."

"When I 'phoned earlier, I asked that the detective constable in charge of the investigation be informed as soon as possible," Stephen quickly added.

"I'm here!" a friendly voice said, as the DC from Stirling appeared on the path behind Jo. He was accompanied by the young constable from Crianlarich police station.

"You two have saved us a lot of further searching," he said warmly. "I've been at Crianlarich station since early morning. Jack here has been most helpful." He indicated the uniformed constable beside him.

Turning to the helpful stranger, who was now looking completely out of his depth and obviously anxious to get on with his walk, the detective said: "Thank you, Sir, for your help. I'll take a brief statement from you first and then let you get off."

He then instructed the three uniformed officers to take their prisoner back to Crianlarich. He would follow as soon as he had obtained statements from the witnesses. "When you get back to the station, arrange for a van to come and pick up the motorcycle," he ended.

The key was handed over, the group departed, and the detective took the young man aside for a few minutes while Stephen and Jo waited uncertainly.

"I hope I did OK," she whispered. "I guessed you wouldn't want to say that our nemesis tried to do us serious injury. I believe we were saved by a miracle, but they'd probably think we were batty!"

Stephen took her hand. "I'm sure you're right. While you were away, I took the liberty of trying to make a bargain with the imposter; we would play down what happened here if he cooperates with the police."

"That was a sensible move," Jo agreed. "I'm glad the uniformed police haven't been told the full story, but we may need to come clean with our friendly detective."

......

When they were alone with the detective and he had quickly written down their short rather bland statements, he closed his notebook and smiled.

"Now is there anything you'd like to tell me off the record?" he asked.

So they told him virtually everything except the miraculous element, stressing only how fortunate they had been not to be hit.

"You're attempt at bargaining may work," the detective said doubtfully. "It certainly did when I tried it with the thug who accosted you but I strongly suspect our Professor is made of sterner stuff. It's a good thing that his accident has shaken him up. If I can't find the SD card you doctored amongst his possessions, it's going to be very hard to charge him with being a central part of this particular theft. That SD card is pretty vital evidence and the wretched man almost certainly realizes it! I'm sorry to say that it may be necessary to summon you two to give evidence against him. It all depends on how well the Thames Valley people manage to sort out their end."

Jo looked a bit stunned at the possibility of being needed as a witness, but Stephen took it in his stride. He also suddenly remembered to tell the detective how the fake professor had found out about their travel plans.

"Yes," Jo added. "He's a very good actor; the poor Stirling landlady would have been putty in his hands!"

"Well, you two can relax now and enjoy the rest of your holiday," the detective replied. "I must be off, but I'm really grateful for all you've done to help avert the loss of some very sensitive information. I'm not allowed to tell you anything more about it; not that I've been told much myself!"

He gave a beaming smile and shook hands with them before disappearing quickly in the direction of the road.

......

"I afraid we've lost almost an hour," Stephen said as they marched quickly onwards. "When we get to Inversnaid Hotel for late lunchtime refreshments, I'll have to 'phone our guesthouse to say we'll not get there much before eight o'clock. We'd better get something to eat before we arrive to save going out again: the nearest pub's in Balmaha!"

"We've got some bananas and chocolate anyway," Jo said cheerfully. "We can tighten our belts if necessary."

"Well, there is a hotel at Rowardennan about seven miles south of Inversnaid. We can drop off there for a late pot of tea and early supper; no need for you to starve after all the day's hard walking! I can also use their Wi-Fi to find accommodation for our last night in or near Milngavie. We've got about 22 miles to walk tomorrow, so it would be risky to leave it until we get there."

......

A mile later, they reached Beinglas Farm, a pleasant-looking campsite with a bar and small shop.

"Excellent!" Stephen said. "I expect you'd like a coffee, but we mustn't be too long; we've covered less than seven miles so far!"

The bar was small but surprisingly pleasant. They were sorry not to be able to stay longer and hurried on after a much-needed hot drink.

The narrow path climbed slowly away from the river through a beautiful landscape and along the flank of a small hill with splendid views of the mountains further east before dropping down again towards some water.

"This is the northern end of Loch Lomond," Stephen announced. "Now for a delightful trek along the eastern bank of the Loch; the notes I made before I left Reading mention climbing up and down steps over huge boulders that have come down from the higher ground to the east!"

"I'm up for a challenge," Jo said enthusiastically. "All our hiking these last few days has increased our fitness no end!"

She did indeed look happy and ready for anything. The fact that Professor Makin was now safely in custody probably has something to do with it, Stephen thought.

A remarkable four miles followed as the path squeezed past enormous boulders, through thickets, and past splendid views out across the Loch. Jo's energy seemed inexhaustible as she scrambled over the frequent outcrops of rock that intercepted the path.

"You were certainly right about the route being a rough one!" she said. "I'm enjoying every minute, but also looking forward to a lunch of some sort; the calories must be burning up at a remarkable rate!"

"We must make the most of the loch views today," Stephen said. "Tomorrow at Balmaha, about 13 miles further south, our route turns east and leaves Loch Lomond completely."

They crossed several streams coming tumbling down into the Loch, and, at one point, climbed up some steps on to a bridge over an impressive chasm where water cascaded down a cliff.

Nevertheless, they were thankful to arrive at the surprisingly large Inversnaid Hotel. Not only was it directly on the West Highland Way but a narrow road brought tourists in from the east.

"This whole area is a paradise for walkers and cyclists," Stephen remarked. "From my map I can see that this road eventually makes its way to Aberfoyle, about 15 miles away."

"I'd agree with the description "paradise" if there were no midges," Jo exclaimed, slapping the side of her face. "My insect repellant has finally given up the unequal struggle!"

......

While having some light refreshments, they took the opportunity to discuss what their priorities should be on returning to Reading.

"There are two main tasks," Stephen said. "Plan the wedding and find a small flat to rent on the outskirts of Swindon, where I'm due to start work at the beginning of September."

"It would be simplest to get married in Pangbourne parish church, if you agree," Jo replied. "Perhaps we could aim for the third Saturday in August. I'm sure my old foster father would be willing to "give me away" and the dear couple will probably offer to have a small buffet reception at their home; they've got a nice garden. I would pay for the food, of course."

"I can contribute to that, as well to some of the other expenses."

"That's kind of you, but there should be no need; I've got that unexpected £1000, unless the police confiscate it as ill-gotten gains! I'll get a simple calf-length white dress that can be dyed afterwards. Alternatively, I could wear a suitable coloured one to start with; all I want is a simple wedding with no frills. After all, we've no family and there'll not be many people there!"

"All I want is to marry you as soon as possible!" Stephen said longingly. "As for finding a flat, we'll have to take several trips to Swindon to look around; it's a good job we've both got bikes."

"I suggest we look for a church first and then find a flat fairly near," Jo said.

"A very sensible idea; cycling to work will be good exercise for me!"

......

It was just on three o'clock when they left the comfortable hotel to continue the hike south along a path that would keep fairly close to the water for most of the seven miles to a very late tea at Rowardennan Hotel, followed by a final three miles on a mixture of path and lane to what looked to Jo, from the pictures she had seen on Stephen's little notebook, like a lovely place for the night.

"We're going to sleep really well after all the excitement and our strenuous exercise today," she thought. "It's not so much the distance we'll have covered but the difficulty of hiking on such a rough path for a large part of the way."

It suddenly occurred to her that she was now thinking less frequently of herself as an individual and much more of Stephen and herself as a couple. "As if I'm already married!" she thought happily, and took the first opportunity that the width of the path allowed to drop back to walk beside her fiancé and take his hand.

116

Stephen glanced at her lovingly before concentrating on the path again. He was thinking about a small leaflet he had picked up in the hotel. It had been on their table; probably left by an earlier guest. The front of the folded sheet of cheap paper asked a single question: "Do you feel like a Stranger?" Intrigued, he had opened it to find a few verses quoted from the end of Chapter 2 of St Paul's letter to the Ephesians, followed by a brief explanation and short prayer.

Not having time to consider it properly, he had slipped the paper in his pocket intending to look at it later with Jo, but a few words had stuck in his memory: "…you are no more strangers and foreigners but fellow citizens……of the household of God…"

As he marched along, these words seemed to be sinking deeper into his consciousness with every step. Although he had made a life-changing decision and knew he was now a Christian, he still did not have the enduring joy and assurance that he knew Jo possessed; she seemed so positive in her new faith. He was sure these words from the Bible were just what he needed.

"Thank you, Jesus, for knowing this all along and giving me this passage describing our brand new status from your perspective," he murmured.

Jo only picked up a few faint words, but she immediately realized that God was doing something special. Seeing that the path was about to get narrower again, she gave her fiancé's hand a loving squeeze of encouragement and speeded up to move in front of him.

Stephen looked at her attractive back view with delight. "She's the most wonderful girl in the world. I'm so in love with her," he thought. "Bumping into her table on the Edinburgh train was the best mistake I ever made!"

Chapter 19: Epilogue

Jo stood at the bedroom window of The Swan Hotel in Streatley gazing out over the Thames; first at the light of the setting sun reflecting off the quiet backwater alongside the hotel terrace and then out over the peaceful stretch of river a few yards upstream from Goring Lock on the opposite bank.

She was wearing a simple light-grey dress that fitted her body perfectly. Stephen had not yet seen it because he had gone into the bathroom for his shower after her. It was almost seven o'clock on a Saturday evening towards the end of August and she was looking forward to dinner, not to mention a two-night honeymoon in the nicest hotel she had ever been in.

It was still hard to believe that she had actually married him nearly seven hours earlier in Pangbourne parish church; she who, as a teenager at secondary school, had once vowed to remain single after having to fend off a succession of amorous boys.

Her first encounter with him had not started auspiciously. She still felt ashamed of herself when she recalled that she had glared angrily at him for spilling some coffee after he had accidentally jogged her table on the train. To make matters worse, he had requested permission to sit opposite her when all she wanted was to be left alone with her worries. Then, quite unknowingly, he had begun to break down her barriers with his sympathy and willingness to assist in solving her dilemma. Of course, all this had been totally eclipsed about four days later when, in quick succession, he had bravely rescued her from being kidnapped, asked her to marry him, and then, almost unbelievably, they had both heard what later transpired to be the voice of the Son of God.

They had never told anyone, with the exception of their dear friend Sarah, the full story of how they became Christians on that hike all the way to Skye; somehow it was too precious to share if it was only going to invite skepticism. They had, however, already begun to share their new-found faith in the seven weeks they had been engaged.

Stephen was now living in the one-bedroom flat they had found together on the outskirts of Swindon quite close to the church they had already attended several times. Although it was an easy journey by train from Pangbourne to Swindon via Reading, being extremely fit, they had both preferred to cycle on their visits to one another. The train had been essential, however, for transferring her modest possessions.

She need not have worried about buying the cheapest and simplest white dress she could find; when she had come up the aisle on her foster father's arm, the look on Stephen's face had calmed any doubts she might have had. At the first opportunity, he had whispered in her ear, "You look totally wonderful!"

After that she was so happy that the day passed almost in a blur: a short but moving service; brief photographs in the churchyard; a happy time circulating amongst friends during the buffet lunch in the garden of her old foster parents; a cheerful send-off on the four-mile drive to Streatley in a car driven by a friend from Goring rowing club; a welcome cup of tea in their delightful bedroom followed by an energetic hour unwinding in the hotel fitness club.

......

Jo was brought out of her reverie by the sound of Stephen's razor in the bathroom. She chuckled quietly; although he had taken great care to have a good shave this morning, he was keeping the promise made a few days ago. "My cheeks and chin will be as smooth as a baby's bottom when we first make love on our wedding night!" he had said, before adding, with a cheeky glance: "I don't promise to keep it like that though!"

Two minutes later he emerged and looked at her in delighted amazement. "My! You were stunning in the white dress. Is it possible that you look even more amazing now? How can you be so beautiful?"

Unable to cope with any more compliments, she ran to him with a little cry of joy and they clung together in one long

119

wonderful kiss before he opened the door and they walked hand-in-hand downstairs to the attractive dining room.

The meal was excellent, but so engrossed were they in each other that they were unable to remember the next day what they had eaten. They lingered at the table with small cups of coffee and then, by unspoken consent, returned upstairs where they partly undressed, cleaned their teeth solemnly, and got ready for bed. Jo normally wore pajamas, but tonight she had a simple nightdress that did not leave much to the imagination.

When she stood shyly beside the bed, Stephen whispered: "In my eyes, you are the loveliest woman in the world!" She flung her arms around his neck with a little sob of joy.